He struck her as a man who would take his pleasures where he found them, and when it suited him. Still, in a crisis he would be tough, intelligent and cold as ice.

'What *is* your own kind?' she couldn't resist asking.

'The sexy, single and preferably silent type,' he answered.

'You left out beautiful—or isn't that important?'

'It's not my priority. Beautiful women play hard to get, and personally I find chasing them a bore.'

'I thought the chase was all.'

'Perhaps that's because you haven't been caught yet!'

MAN ON THE MAKE

BY

ROBERTA LEIGH

MILLS & BOON LIMITED
ETON HOUSE   18-24 PARADISE ROAD
RICHMOND   SURREY   TW9 1SR

*First published in Great Britain 1989
by Mills & Boon Limited*

© Scribe Associates 1989

*Australian copyright 1989
Philippine copyright 1989
This edition 1989*

ISBN 0 263 76380 3

*Set in English Times 11 on 12 pt.
05 – 8910 – 44404*

Typeset in Great Britain by JCL Graphics, Bristol

Made and Printed in Great Britain

CHAPTER ONE

As Mark Rayner heard what his next assignment was to be, he was hard pressed not to hand in his resignation there and then.

'I didn't join Intelligence to play nursemaid to a spoilt little rich girl, sir,' he said crisply.

'Don't talk in clichés,' Sir Elrick Watson reproved mildly. 'If this job weren't more than that, I wouldn't be asking you to handle it.'

'It's her father who should be doing so.'

Even as he made the comment, Mark knew he was allowing hope to get the better of reason. While the safety of Charlotte Beauville was not of major importance to the West, it was significant enough to warrant her protection—which was why he had brought the matter to the attention of his superior in the first place. But he had not anticipated being asked to supervise the operation himself.

'I assume the facts in here are correct?' Sir Elrick tapped the file in front of him.

'Absolutely. The CIA have been watching General Vargar for months, and he's already left the capital and moved into the hills.'

'But they're certain they know what he's up to?'

'Yes,' Mark said firmly. 'Teleguay is ripe for revolution, and the moment it happens, Vargar's

5

men will attempt to hold Miss Beauville hostage.'

'Her father refuses to believe it.'

'He's aware of the situation, surely?'

The older man shrugged. 'When your mining interests in a country give employment to thousands, you may be forgiven for thinking no citizen in their right mind would wish to harm you or your family. Anyway, Beauville says he's been protecting his daughter for twenty-three years without help from any damned government agency—his words, not mine—and he sees no reason to change things.'

'There's a world of difference between protecting your daughter from kidnappers only interested in money, and trigger-happy terrorists.'

'You'll have to convince Beauville of that. And quickly, too. If the rebels get their hands on the girl, it could have unpleasant repercussions for the West.'

Mark knew Sir Elrick was right, but it didn't make him any happier with his task. For the next few months it looked as if he'd be committed to watching over a spoilt young woman who'd probably resent having him around as much as he resented being there.

'I'll catch the next available flight to Nice,' he said. 'I take it Beauville's expecting me?'

'Yes. I called him as soon as I decided you were the best man for the job.'

'What about French Security? As Beauville now lives in France, won't their noses be out of joint if they aren't called in?'

'The man's a British subject,' Sir Elrick replied, as if that were answer enough, and Mark pulled a face.

'Pity. Guarding a spoilt beauty is more to Gallic tastes than British!'

The smile which accompanied his words lit up his lean face and briefly revealed strong, white teeth. Tall and broad-shouldered, he more closely resembled the rugger blue he had been at Oxford twelve years ago than the highly placed Intelligence Officer he had now become. Indeed, many of his friends, believing him to be something or other in the Foreign Office, felt he had let his country down by not pursuing a career in sport. But two things had prevented him: an exceptionally high IQ which required mental challenge—as opposed to mainly physical—and a deep fund of common sense which made him regard all sport as play.

Separately these attributes might not have brought him success, but the two together added up to a man of formidable strength of character, and while still at university he had been recruited by Sir Elrick.

Soon after obtaining his degree he had dropped out of sight for a year. No one other than his immediate family knew where he had gone, and when he finally surfaced he was thinner and tougher, his mind and body honed to a fine precision. Women of all ages fell over themselves to attract him, and he took what they offered, satisfied them physically, but gave away nothing of his inner self. His work was his life, and because of it he eschewed emotional ties.

'I'll keep you informed of developments, sir,' he said now. 'But I'll have to play it by ear.'

'Suits me,' Sir Elrick smiled. 'Your ear's better than Menuhin's!'

Four hours later, Mark was crossing the hot tarmac of Nice airport, forefinger looped through the jacket flung over his shoulder. The Mediterranean sky was a cloudless blue, the air as warm and soft on his skin as the hand of a pampered woman. Watching several formally attired businessmen with briefcases walking alongside him, he thought how out of place they were.

This was the coast of the rich and idle: the jet setters who concentrated their energies on enjoying themselves. Which brought him back to Charlotte Beauville. His mouth thinned. It was unfair to judge her before they met, but from what he had gleaned she was no different from the other empty-headed beauties who Concorded here and there in a haze of Arpège and Dom Pérignon.

'Negresco,' he told the taxi driver with the automatic caution that came from rigid training, and lounged back in his seat as if his only interest was in pleasure, like the crowds thronging the stony beach alongside the Promenade des Anglais.

Half an hour later he was in another taxi, retracing his journey as he headed in the direction of Antibes, one of the prettiest towns on the Riviera. Satisfied he was not being followed, he instructed the driver to take him to the Cap, the promontory beyond the town, where Charles Beauville had his estate.

It occupied the end of a smaller promontory that jutted out like a ragged finger from the larger bulk of the Cap. On three sides the grounds ended at the cliff's edge, almost vertical walls leading down to a craggy shoreline too rocky to be used by bathers. That left only the landward side to be guarded. Mark eyed the seven-foot-high wall—electrified, no doubt—which ran for nearly a quarter of a mile. It seemed impregnable, but experience had taught him that nothing should be taken for granted.

The driver stopped outside a pair of massive iron gates, guarded by a tough-looking man in a bullet-proof box. Speaking into the intercom set in the wall, Mark gave his name, and a moment later his taxi was bowling along a winding drive shaded by firs. The villa, when it finally came in sight, was a glorious Technicolour shock to the eye.

Cream-walled and red-tiled, it stood in a blaze of golden light, blue sky and emerald lawns. Narrow marble columns supported the arched lintel overhanging the front door, and this Moorish aspect was reflected in the half-moon architraves above the windows. These were gracefully marked by slatted-wood shutters, painted a soft terracotta; some were open, but most were closed, as if to preserve the interior from prying eyes.

Mark waited until the taxi was out of sight before pressing the front door bell, and almost at once it was opened by a white-jacketed man with impassive oriental features.

'Please come this way, Mr Rayner,' he said. 'Mr Beauville is expecting you.'

Mark stepped into the hall. Large and circular, one section of the wall was covered by an exquisite tapestry, while on the right a wide marble staircase with polished bronze handrail swept up to the first floor. Beyond the stairs he glimpsed the library, the furniture dark but relieved by ormolu trim. The best of French Empire, he decided, and wondered if the rest of the house was as predictable.

It wasn't. The enormous living-room ahead—sliding glass doors composing the wall facing the terrace—was American modern at its most subtle. It did not have the feel of an interior decorator's hand, either—the style was too personal—and he wondered whether it was the father's or daughter's.

Whichever, it abounded with *objets d'art* and paintings worth a king's ransom, and it was these which held his attention. As he moved around the room, savouring a Corot, a Rembrandt, a Holbein, the golden-haired Labrador he had seen as he entered padded over to sniff at his legs.

'Some guard dog!' Mark said aloud, bending to fondle the velvety ears. 'I could have had a canvas off the wall, replaced it with a forgery, and all you'd have done is lick my hand!'

'Try it,' a quiet voice said behind him, and Mark swung round to see Charles Beauville.

His appearance did little to signify he was one of the world's richest men. Thin and short, with carefully combed, sparse grey hair, he could best be described as neat and dapper. His beige linen safari suit did not flatter his sallow complexion, and his hands, one holding an unlit cigar, were heavily veined. But, if his appearance gave the impression of age, it was dispelled by the firmness of his clasp and the brightness of the deep-set eyes behind gold-rimmed glasses.

'Sandy may look harmless,' the man went on, 'but make a sudden move and he'll have you in a grasp tighter than a Japanese wrestler!' He moved towards a well-stocked trolley. 'Care for a drink before we start talking?'

'Thanks. A fruit juice, please.'

Charles Beauville filled two glasses, then waved Mark to an armchair before seating himself opposite. For a moment he regarded the younger man—then, apparently satisfied, he leaned back, visibly relaxing.

'Sir Elrick's given me the facts,' he stated, 'and I think it only fair to say I don't take them seriously. You Intelligence fellows are inclined to make mountains out of molehills.'

'There's no reason why we should.' Mark tried to curb his impatience. 'We've more than enough real problems on our hands without inventing any.'

'I'm not saying you're fabricating—simply over-reacting.'

Mark decided not to pull his punches. 'If the rebels win control of Teleguay, they believe that a major industrialist such as yourself could persuade the West that all the natural resources in their country should belong to the state, and not foreign companies. And for a start, they'd get you to hand over all your mining concessions there.'

'As a philanthropic gesture to an emerging nation, you mean?' came the ironic question.

'Yes. And General Vargar will hold your daughter hostage until you do so.'

The magnate was silent for a long moment. 'You've made out a good case, Rayner,' he said finally. 'You'd better tell me what extra security I should take for her.'

'Nothing obvious. We don't want to alert Vargar's men that we're on to them. But I'd like someone who's trained for this kind of situation, to be with her the entire time.'

'Such as yourself?' Charles Beauville was quick on the uptake.

'Do you have any objection, sir?'

'Of course not—but my daughter will. She's always resented the idea of a personal minder.'

'She'll think differently when you tell her the position.'

'I've no intention of worrying her with it.'

Clearly her father spoilt her to distraction, Mark thought, recalling from Beauville's dossier that his wife had died when their daughter was five.

'It's up to you, sir,' he said aloud. 'But how can I stay close to her unless she knows who I am?'

'We're in luck there. Roberts—her chauffeur—is retiring and I've been hunting around for a replacement. I don't engage her personal staff without her approval, so she'll have to vet you herself. Make sure you have a convincing background ready, and try to disguise that upper-class accent of yours!' There was an unexpected twinkle in the brown eyes. 'You're clearly more used to giving orders than taking them, so this job won't be easy for you. My daughter can be headstrong when the mood takes her.' He came a step closer. 'Good luck, Rayner. You're going to need it!'

The man disappeared and Mark replenished his glass from a silver pitcher of fruit juice, then wandered out to the garden. Rolling lawns stretched down to the cliff's edge, where a four-foot-high rail was protection against the sharp descent to the sea which washed on the rocks below.

On the right, some thirty yards from the house, stone steps led down the cliff, and he strolled over to see where they ended. On a terrace below, blue and gold tiles surrounded a vast, kidney-shaped swimming pool. A diving-board raised its head at one end, while at the other stood a Grecian-style pavilion. Changing-rooms, he assumed, and probably a sauna and bar.

He wondered if Charles Beauville took advantage of this mogul-size recreation area. Somehow he didn't think so. It was simply another expensive toy for his daughter's amusement.

Returning to the terrace bordering the villa, he sat down and waited for the girl to appear. The Labrador wandered out, regarded him with what seemed like a smile, then flopped at his feet.

Mark glanced at his watch. Beauville had been almost half an hour, so where was his daughter? Having a siesta? The heat was certainly sleep-inducing, and Mark felt an urge to close his eyes. He was one of the fortunate few who could cat-nap and wake as refreshed as if he had had a full night's sleep. He leaned back against the floral cushions, and suppressed a yawn. He'd better stay alert. A chauffeur wasn't likely to nod off while waiting to be interviewed!

'Sorry to have kept you,' a husky voice said behind him, and Mark jumped to his feet as a tall, slender girl glided towards him.

'Mark Rayner,' he introduced himself, extending his hand.

Ignoring it, she appraised him as diligently as a housewife inspecting a side of beef. 'Do take off your jacket,' she said laconically. 'You must be boiling in this heat.'

'That's all right, miss.' Mark mentally kicked himself for proffering his hand. 'I'm used to it.'

'At least sit down.'

He did so, trying to appear deferential. The girl perched on the edge of a wrought-iron table, gently swinging one long, shapely leg. Her white linen shirt and trousers were understated and casual, but clearly expensive. Everything about her spoke of careful grooming and a pampered, easy life. Her complexion was clear, the red-gold hair in careful disarray, the greeny-gold eyes framed by preposterously long lashes. She was bra-less, her breasts firm and perfectly shaped, and he was certain she was flaunting the fact. Purposely he kept his eyes on her face and, noting the firm chin and direct gaze, guessed she was as strong-willed as her father had intimated.

'Daddy says you have excellent references, and that your last job was with Sir Elrick somebody or other. Why did you leave?'

'I had to do a lot of overtime and didn't get paid extra for it.'

This was nearer the truth than the girl would ever know, Mark thought wryly. But one didn't go into Intelligence for the money, and he had relied on his wits to supplement his income. With the same mixture of shrewdness and courage that had saved his life on many occasions, he had turned a small inheritance from his grandparents into a sizeable fortune which enabled him to live exactly as he wished. Not that his family were poor. On the contrary. But he had always insisted on making his own way.

'You won't have a nine-to-five job here, either,' the girl broke into his thoughts.

'I know. But your father's offering a generous salary.'

'He thinks money buys loyalty.'

'Don't you, miss?'

'No. Bought loyalty only lasts until a better offer comes along. You illustrate my point exactly!'

'I have to earn the best living I can.' Mark endeavoured to appear anxious. 'I hope you'll engage me?'

'You're rather young for the post.'

'I'm an excellent driver.'

'I took that for granted.' She regarded him speculatively. 'Are you good at sport?'

'It depends which.'

'Not darts,' she said rudely.

Mark resisted the urge to slap her. 'I swim and play tennis, if that's what you mean.'

'Good. I think you'll do, Rayner. It might be fun having someone young around.' She sauntered towards the living-room, then paused and looked over her shoulder. 'My father said you're free to start tomorrow, so I'll expect you then. Roberts will explain your duties to you, and until he leaves, please keep in the background.'

'We haven't spoken about time off,' Mark said.

'That will be at *my* convenience. But I'll try to let you know in advance.'

'Good of you, miss.'

She gave him a sharp look, and he knew he had to watch his tongue. The girl was no fool, and he didn't want to give himself away in case she acted the prima donna and refused to have him around.

'Where do I go for my uniform?' Adroitly he side-tracked.

'Roberts will take you to the tailor you will use, but meanwhile navy trousers and pale blue shirt will do.'

Without another word she was gone, and Mark breathed more easily. Charlotte Beauville was a thoroughly spoiled bitch who wouldn't be easy to handle.

Still, he'd take orders up to a point, though he had no intention of being a pet pooch who came to heel at the snap of 'my lady's' fingers!

CHAPTER TWO

CHARLOTTE lay in bed, wondering why she was miserable. Then she remembered. Roberts was leaving today, a week earlier than she had expected.

'No point having Rayner here doing nothing,' her father had said last night, and Charlotte, seeing the logic of the statement, had not argued.

She had known for months that Roberts was retiring, but had put it from her mind. He had been with her since she was ten, and she would never find anyone she liked or trusted as much. Certainly not Rayner, for though he appeared competent and dependable there was something about him that puzzled her: an air of supreme confidence, conceit almost, a strength and self-assurance which had nothing to do with machismo, but clearly indicated he would be happier giving orders than taking them.

He was undeniably attractive, too, and must be used to being chased by women. She wouldn't be surprised if many of his conquests had been his employer's wives and daughters! Her full mouth tightened. From the assessing manner in which he had eyed her when he'd thought she wasn't looking, he probably figured she'd be a pushover, too! Well, he was in for a surprise. She would make him dance to *her* tune, treat him as she would never have treated

18

Roberts.

It was an amusing prosepect. Since childhood she had been taught to respect everyone who worked for her. Indeed, it had never occurred to her to do otherwise—until now, when she decided it would be fun to put Mark Rayner in his place—and keep him there!

There was a knock on the door, and her maid entered to draw the curtains and run her bath. Normally Charlotte encouraged Maria to stay and chat, but today she wanted to be alone with her thoughts. Pushing aside the blue satin sheets that toned with the décor, she padded into the bathroom, her tall, slender body moving with unconscious grace, her luxuriant red-gold hair rippling to her shoulders like a fall of autumn leaves.

Reaching for her brush, she stroked it through the silken strands. The colour was a legacy from her mother. Irish, to match her temper, her father always said, reminding her of the dual sides to her nature, the practical from his Belgian ancestry, the artistic from the Emerald Isle. Twisting her hair into a knot atop her head, she stepped into the sunken marble tub.

Relaxing in the scented water, she mused on her new chauffeur, pretty sure her father had chosen him because he could use a gun as expertly as he drove a car. Throughout her life, her father had tried to hide the fact that she was constantly guarded, and she had never had the heart to tell him she knew perfectly well what was going on. Even now, he didn't think she realised that many of the gardeners were actually security men!

Wrapping herself in a fluffy towelling robe, she returned to the bedroom and pressed a button set into the wall. Mirrored doors slid back to reveal a walk-in wardrobe, fifteen feet square, where her summer clothes and accessories were set out in perfect order. Several dozen bikinis were neatly stacked on a shelf, and she chose one at random. It was hyacinth blue and deepened her creamy skin—not that it bothered her how she looked today. She wasn't seeing anyone, unless one counted the new chauffeur, and her interest in him was strictly professional.

Mark Rayner, feeling refreshed and at ease in pale blue shirt and dark blue trousers, the uniform worn by the male servants in the household, was standing at the foot of the curving staircase when her High and Mightiness came sauntering down, her short robe—belted loosely around her tiny waist—parting to reveal long, shapely legs.

'Good morning,' he said deferentially.

'Good morning, Rayner.'

Her expression was as cool as her tone. Going to put me in my place, he thought with amusement, and was careful to hide his smile.

'I'm having breakfast on the terrace,' she went on. 'I'll call you when I need you.'

She walked past him, the edge of her robe brushing his arm as she made no effort to avoid him, the gesture clearly indicating *he* was the one who should step out of the way. Quickly he did, and headed for the staff sitting-room.

It was empty, and he went down the narrow passage

to the magnificently equipped kitchen. Yvette, the cook, greeted him warmly, his fluent French having endeared him to her, and she gave him a cup of coffee and a chunk of warm *brioche*, lavishly buttered.

Straddling a chair, he bit into the bread, murmuring appreciatively as he did so. By nature averse to gossip, his Intelligence training had taught him the importance of being friendly with staff, who generally knew more of the goings-on in a house than their employers gave them credit for. But even more important in this instance was his fear that the Teleguayans had infiltrated the household to gain information on Charlotte's movements, and he was trying to assess how each employee felt about her.

'Miss Charlotte's spoilt, of course,' Yvette replied in answer to his skilful pumping, 'but she has a good heart. When my ankles are bad—I've terrible arthritis—she always pops into my room for a chat.'

'How long have you known her?'

'Since she was five. The year her mother died. She was such a happy little girl until then. Mrs Beauville always cared for her daughter herself, you know. They'd waited years for a child, and when Miss Charlotte arrived they doted on her.'

'No wonder she's spoiled,' Mark commented, anxious to keep the conversation flowing.

'She only became headstrong and self-willed when the nurses and governesses took over. It was their authority against hers, and she usually won.'

Yvette droned on and Mark stored everything, hoping the day wouldn't come when *he* had to exert authority over this young heiress. If he did, the fur would certainly fly!

Charlotte, glancing through the papers as she ate, noticed the usual idiotic references to herself. She'd have to be Superwoman to be in so many places at once, or be accompanied by so many different escorts! The fact that for the past few months she had only been dating Barry Davenport, heir to Davenport Steel, wasn't even mentioned.

'Going out or spending the day here?' Her father stopped beside her chair and placed an affectionate hand on her cheek.

'Here,' she smiled. 'Barry may come over later, and a few of the crowd are dropping by for drinks.'

'Have a good day, then, sweetheart. I've a meeting in Rome and will spend the night there.' Dropping a kiss on her head, he walked briskly away.

Charlotte gathered together the novel she was reading and a gold leather bag that matched her thonged sandals, and strolled down to the pool. The heat was already intense and she settled herself on a sun-lounger, slipped off her robe and opened her book.

It was top of the best-seller list, but after a few pages she found the story stereotyped and, flinging it aside, rolled on to her stomach and unfastened the top of her bikini. Her breasts, full and firm, flattened slightly as she lay on them, and she adjusted her position to a more comfortable one.

'Your father asked me to join you.'

With a gasp, Charlotte raised her head to see Mark Rayner in front of her. 'You startled me,' she said crossly. 'I didn't see you coming.'

But she was seeing him now, and he was well worth a look. Brief black swimming-trunks clung to him like a second skin, drawing attention to his muscular legs and strong thighs. His shoulders were wide and powerful, the triangular tangle of hair she had glimpsed through his shirt thick and silky, the sheen of his lightly bronzed skin owing nothing to oil.

'I didn't mean to give you a fright,' he apologised.

'I wasn't frightened, merely annoyed. No one will snatch me away down here.' She fastened her bikini top. 'Do you know the weekly food bills for the guard dogs could feed an average family for a month?'

'I'm sure your father considers the expenditure worth while,' Mark said tonelessly.

'Well, I don't.'

'You mean you don't think you're in any danger?'

'I'm not stupid! But I'm sure there's no need for a machine gun behind every bush or a "minder" disguised as a chauffeur. You don't fool me, Rayner. Genuine chauffeurs don't wear shoulder-holsters under their jackets.'

If she had hoped to impress him with her powers of deduction, she was disappointed, for he merely looked amused.

'Have you always done this sort of work?' she asked.

He shook his head, and a lock of silky dark hair

fell forward. He raked it back with a strong, well-kept hand. 'I'm best described as a jack of all trades.'

'And master of all, too,' she commented drily. 'I assume that's why my father hired you.'

'I think he was impressed by my references, miss.'

'I'd give anything to lead a normal life,' Charlotte muttered, ignoring his remark. 'It's so depressing being cocooned from the real world, not free to go where I want, see whom I choose. Even at college I wasn't allowed to live on campus because my father didn't think it safe.'

'What did you study?'

'Fine Arts.'

'Very appropriate, considering your father's fame as a collector. Do you buy for him?'

'Not if he can help it!' she grinned. 'Our tastes are completely different. He goes in for Old Masters, while I prefer discovering young ones!' She twined a red-gold curl around her finger, and the gesture—with gold bracelets on the slender wrist—was unconsciously sensual. 'Discovering new talent and helping it along financially is my hobby.'

'An admirable one,' Rayner answered.

'My father thinks I should be doing something more active—preferably in his business—but I can't work up any enthusiasm for it.'

'Who will eventually take over from him?'

'He has dozens of directors.'

'But, to paraphrase Harry Truman, where will

the buck stop?'

'With the man I marry, I suppose. He's certain to be a millionaire in his own right—and won't be able to resist the opportunity of becoming a billionaire in *my* right!' She gave a wry smile. 'Which means I'll be exchanging one kind of prison for another.'

'At least the bars will be diamond-studded!'

'I don't find that amusing,' she sniffed. 'I don't even know why I've told you all this.'

'I appreciate the confidence, Miss Beauville,' he said instantly, 'and I sympathise with you.'

'Enough to allow me some freedom?' she asked at once.

'I'm afraid that isn't up to me.'

'I'm quite capable of taking care of myself,' she snorted. 'I'm a judo black-belt, and can shoot as well as any man here—present company excluded, of course,' she added sarcastically. 'We'll have to arrange a competition and have a bet on the outcome.' Lithely she swung into a sitting position. 'Are you a betting man, Rayner?'

'I enjoy a flutter. But I'd better warn you, I'm a lucky gambler.'

'Then perhaps I'll play safe and put my money on *you*!'

His laugh was spontaneous and she liked the sound of it; liked what it did to his face too, taking away the watchful air and softening the features. Relaxed, his mouth was fuller and nicely curved. Even his eyes altered, creasing at the corners and turning their steely dark grey to silver. She caught her breath irritably. What did it matter what he looked like? He wasn't her boyfriend!

'I'm going for a swim,' she said abruptly. 'Please go to the house and fetch me another bikini. I don't want to sit around in a wet one.'

'I'd rather not leave you,' he replied. 'I'll phone and ask your maid to bring one down.'

'Are you refusing to do as I asked?' Charlotte had reached the steps of the pool and whirled round to face him.

'Of course not, but——'

'Then do it! You'll find them in my walk-in wardrobe.'

Without waiting for his answer, she lowered herself into the water, and when she turned round again he had gone.

As Mark strode towards the villa his eyes scanned the lawns. Stop being paranoid, he chided himself. He had checked the guard points himself and couldn't fault one of them. Excellent hide-outs and excellent men. Yet he was nervous as a cat. Out of practice with this sort of work, that was the trouble. This assignment should have been given to someone in Security.

Before going to Charlotte Beauville's room, he snatched a moment to call Sir Elrick.

'Mark! Glad to hear from you.' The voice was clipped. 'We've just had word that the rebels have won control of Teleguay.'

'So I'm in for a long stay here, then?'

'Unless Beauville lets us put his daughter in a safe house for the next few months.'

'Forget it, sir. Even if her father agrees, she won't.'

'Like that, eh?'

'I'm afraid so. She wants to be regarded as an ordinary girl.'

'I wish to heaven she were!'

'Me, too,' Mark rejoined with feeling. 'If she carries on as she has this morning, she'll be needing protection from *me*.'

There was a whoop of laughter. 'Good for your self-control, my boy. You haven't had to exercise it enough where women are concerned!'

'That isn't quite what I meant.'

'Oh?' Sir Elrick replied. 'Then I'm not with you.'

'You're lucky,' Mark sighed, and put down the receiver.

Charlotte waited impatiently for Rayner to return. She had discarded her wet bikini, and the minuscule pieces of silk were hanging out to dry on the wooden-slatted foot-rest. Wrapped in a pink towelling robe that revealed almost as much as it concealed, and with her long, red-gold hair pinned roughly atop her head, she knew she was infinitely desirable.

Not that Rayner seemed aware of it. He stood in front of her as immobile as a statue, not a flicker of an eyelid showing any response to her near nakedness.

'Your bikini, miss.' He held it out to her.

'You didn't exactly hurry yourself,' she muttered.

'I was waylaid by one of the maids. She was checking to see if I had everything I wanted in my room.'

'Do you?'

'Yes, thank you, miss. Your father is most considerate.'

'*I'm* most considerate,' she said haughtily. 'My father leaves the running of the house to me.'

'Then you do an excellent job, miss.'

His tone was humble, though his expression made her suspect he didn't mean it. Her eyes fell on the two strips of polka-dotted silk still in her hand, and her face clouded with anger.

'They don't match! You've brought me the top of one bikini and the bottom of another.'

'I'm sorry, miss, I didn't realise. I'm colour-blind, you see.'

Charlotte wasn't sure whether to believe him, but for the moment had little choice. She'd discover the truth eventually, and heaven help him if he'd been lying!

'Why didn't you say so?' she asked aloud.

'You didn't give me a chance. You insisted I did as I was told.'

He was right and she knew it, but she had no intention of apologising to him. 'Well, you can go back and ask Maria to sort out the right costume.'

Silently he went off, but for some reason Charlotte did not feel she had scored a victory over him, but rather had been taught a lesson by a master tactician.

CHAPTER THREE

CHARLOTTE had lunch by the pool, and Mark Rayner, eating French bread and cheese behind a clump of bushes—he had been unwilling to go to the staff dining-room and leave his charge alone for so long—watched in amazement as she downed a Charentais melon, lobster salad, and a huge bowl of fresh raspberries and cream.

'It's nice to see a woman who doesn't pick at her food,' he commented as he rejoined her a little later, then caught himself up, realising it was hardly the remark one should make to one's employer. She didn't seem to mind, however, for her wide-apart green eyes crinkled with amusement.

'How about you, Rayner? Do you count calories?'

'Never.'

'Then Yvette will love you and pile your plate high!'

'I'll have to make certain I get plenty of exercise.'

'You can have a swim now, if you wish,' Charlotte Beauville suggested. 'If you're worried about deserting your post, you'll find a choice of new swimming trunks in the pool-house. So you won't have to wear wet ones afterwards.'

'I took the liberty of leaving a spare pair of my own in one of the lockers,' he said, and, seeing finely arched eyebrows rise haughtily, quickly added, 'I planned on a dawn swim or a late-night one.'

She gestured dismissively and, trying to look suitably grateful, he went in search of a towel.

When he returned to the pool, the girl was stretched out on her mattress, her eyes closed. Slowly he studied her. Not a fault to be discerned in her beautiful body. She was long-limbed and slender as a doe, yet with all the right curves and beautiful breasts. Had they met in the normal course of events . . . His eyes went to her hair, glowing like fire and quite different from Lisa's, the raven-haired beauty who had shared his last vacation in Bermuda and was still pursuing him.

He padded across the marble tiles and stopped a yard from the mattress. A moment passed, then another. He knew she wasn't asleep—the flicker of her eyes beneath her lids told him that—and he longed to pick her up and shake her. Or smack her smartly where it would hurt most! Still, two could play the same game and, motionless, he remained where he was.

After another moment the slender shoulders lifted and greeny-gold eyes squinted against the sunlight. Mark felt himself surveyed flagrantly from head to toe. Undressed too, he didn't doubt! He guessed Charlotte was testing him, waiting to see if she could excite or embarrass him with her near nakedness. But any hopes she might have had were dashed, for he was too well-trained to give his feelings away. Indifferently he sauntered over to the diving-board. She had asked if he was a good swimmer, and he would give her a demonstration.

Steadily he climbed to the topmost rung and took up his position at the edge of the board, feeling its spring beneath his feet. The muscles in his stomach tensed as he raised his arms, lowered his head and dived. It was a perfect one and he entered the water clean as a knife. His hands touched the bottom of the pool and he glided slowly to the surface and swam in a strong crawl to the side.

With a lithe gesture he levered himself out and sat on the edge, aware of Charlotte watching him. He waited for her to speak, and was irritated when she silently turned over on her stomach. Rude bitch!

Quietly he settled himself a little distance from her and lay back. His irritation turned to amusement. If she expected him to show pique, she'd have a long wait. He sensed rather than heard her stand up, her feet making a barely perceptible sound as she passed him.

Charlotte had deliberately not praised Rayner's dive, deciding he was conceited enough, and as she climbed the diving-board she was aware of him watching her. Confident that anything he could do she could do equally well—she had not been coached by an Olympic champion for nothing!—she performed a backward somersault, landing in the water with the barest splash.

'Excellent, miss,' he called. 'I've never seen better. Really first class.'

She knew instantly that his praise, twice repeated, was intended to show up her own lack of manners when she had watched *his* dive, and she flushed angrily. How dared he try to put her in her place?

Returning to her mattress, she found it impossible to relax. Annoyingly, Rayner had no such difficulty, and within a moment his regular breathing told her he had fallen asleep.

Cautiously she propped herself on an elbow and surveyed him. Lying flat, his thick hair fell away from his forehead, auburn lights glinting among the brown. Lines ran down either side of his long, narrow nose to his mouth, but they were only faint ones, and his wide brow was smooth.

Even in repose he looked a man to be reckoned with, a man well able to take care of himself—and her. Then why the hell wasn't he? Why was he sleeping when he should be alert? Even as she thought this, his eyes flew open, bright as a bird's, and she hurriedly jumped to her feet.

'Fancy a game of tennis?' she asked.

'Isn't it too hot?'

'Not for me.'

With an acquiescent shrug, he rose. 'I don't have the proper gear with me, miss.'

'You'll find what you need in the changing-room next to the court,' she told him, leading the way towards it.

When he emerged, casually smart in white shorts and top bearing the magical YSL label, she had already changed into a pleated sundress. Silently she went straight to the far end of the court, not bothering to observe the accepted etiquette of tossing for sides. Let *him* face the sun, she decided mutinously. He had as good as told her she lacked manners, so why bother to disprove it?

Hitting a ball across to him, they knocked up for the next two minutes.

'Let's start,' she called out impatiently. 'It's boring tapping the ball back and forth. I'll toss for service.'

'Are you sure you want to bother?'

His expression was bland, but she wasn't fooled, and swallowing her chagrin she spun her racket. 'Rough or smooth?'

'Rough.'

'Your serve,' she said, childishly peeved at losing, and unable to hide it.

She crouched low and his ball smashed across the net, a perfect ace which she had no chance of returning. So he intended playing all out, did he? If his service was anything to go by, she had more than met her match.

He won the opening set six-one, and half-way through the second she began to wilt. But she had no intention of giving in. Face flushed, red-gold hair flying in the bright sunlight, she rushed for every ball, beads of perspiration glinting on her face and between the cleft of her breasts.

She threw a swift glance at Rayner. Chauffeur? Not only was he always where he should be, lobbing at the net, top-spinning at impossible-to-return angles, but he looked as cool as a cucumber! Reluctantly she acknowledged the power of his play and the sheer physical attraction of him.

Yet, with the tenacity of someone who hated to lose, she gave the game her all. It was a hopeless battle, though, and he trounced her well and truly.

'You put up a good fight,' he conceded as they left the court.

'You're pretty neat yourself.'

'Who taught you?' he asked, and grinned when she named a Wimbledon champion. 'I should have known!'

'My father believes in the best.'

The chauffeur said nothing.

'Do you only speak when you're spoken to, Rayner?'

'This is my first day, miss. I'm feeling my way.'

'Does that mean you'll be more talkative in future?'

'If that's what you wish, miss.'

'Right now, I wish you'd stop "missing" at the end of every sentence! Subservience doesn't suit you.'

'Really, miss? Sorry, that slipped out.'

'I don't think you're in the least sorry,' Charlotte rejoined. 'I think you're putting on an act. It's the first thing I noticed about you. You don't fit the part.'

'If you find me impertinent, I——'

'Not impertinent, Rayner, I wouldn't stand for that, but there's something about you . . .' She disappeared into one of the changing-rooms, indicating he should do the same.

Mark emerged first, positive that when Charlotte reappeared she'd resume her attack on him. He was proved right, for as she joined him she asked how old he was.

'I'm thirty-two.'

'Where were you born?' she persisted as they returned to the poolside. 'Dad didn't show me your references. He said he'd given them back to you.'

'I come from Oxfordshire.'

'The stockbroker belt?'

'Hardly. Our part was the pawnbroker belt!'

She chuckled. 'What does your father do?'

'He's retired. But he was regular army.' Mark hoped his tone indicated the lower ranks rather than the general he had been!

'And your mother?'

'She sews.' Well, that was no lie; last year a gallery had shown the exquisite tapestries she created.

'Any brothers and sisters?'

'One of each. My brother runs a smallholding.' That was true, too, for it *was* small compared with the thousands of acres his brother-in-law owned!

'And your sister?'

'She's married and lives miles from civilisation.' Mark thought of Alison in her Scottish castle, surrounded by dogs and children and a doting husband she adored.

'Let's get back to you.' Charlotte perched by the pool and dangled her legs in the glittering water. 'Where did you learn to speak such good French? I overheard you talking to one of the staff.'

'I used to accompany my previous employer abroad, and we frequently came over here.'

'I see. I thought perhaps you'd gone to university.'

'Oh, no, miss,' Mark lied. 'I'm not a great one for learning.'

'Don't talk yourself down, Rayner. You strike me as being rather bright. And you certainly talk well—content as well as accent.'

I'm not the only one who's bright, he reflected amusedly, knowing one slip could blow his cover. 'I'm a good mimic,' he said aloud, 'and working for clever people has taught me a lot.'

'Don't you resent being at someone's beck and call?'

'Very few of us are totally free. Anyway, I enjoy living in luxurious surroundings, driving expensive cars and travelling the world first class—and being paid for it into the bargain!'

'Ever thought of becoming a gigolo?' she asked rudely. 'It's the perfect occupation for a good-looking man who doesn't fancy hard work. You might even end up with a proposal of marriage!'

'I'd never give up my freedom for mere money.'

'Would you give it up for love?'

'Not as long as I can get it without tying myself down!'

'Then you'll be single for years!' she said tartly, sliding into the water. 'Come in and cool off.'

'That's an order I'll enjoy obeying! Care to race me to the end? I'll give you a few yards' start.'

'You're on.'

They both struck out, and he allowed her to get a fair distance ahead before overtaking and passing her.

'Don't worry,' he grinned when she finally reached the side and hauled herself up on the ledge beside him. 'You'll beat most women hollow.'

Hearing the compliment, Charlotte was delighted, then instantly annoyed with herself for being affected by anything he said.

'Is there any sport you aren't good at, Rayner?'

'Netball.'

She couldn't help laughing. 'I think you've put me in my place enough for one day. You can have the rest of it off. I won't need you till to-morrow.'

'Are you in this evening, then?'

'Even if I'm not, I shan't be going out alone.'

'Your father says I must accompany you at all times.'

'You're *my* chauffeur, and you'll take orders from *me*, she said irritably.

'I take orders from whoever's paying me,' Rayner replied. 'And that's your father.'

Rayner's attitude brooked no argument, and though she was boiling with rage Charlotte considered it less hassle to give in. When she saw her father, she'd make her feelings clear. She might even have this bumptious upstart dismissed!

'As a matter of fact, I won't be going out,' she said. 'I'm having a few people over, so you're free to do as you like. But if you do intend being around, stay in the background and don't chat up my girlfriends.'

She was delighted to see the colour creep into his face, though his answer brought the colour to hers.

'I wouldn't dream of it, Miss Beauville, any more than I'd dream of chatting *you* up. I know my place.'

'Do you? It's not always apparent.'

'I'm sorry if I occasionally speak frankly. But I assure you that when it comes to women, I prefer to stick to my own kind.'

Charlotte didn't believe him. He struck her as a man who would take his pleasures where he found them, and when it suited him. Still, in a crisis he would be tough, intelligent and cold as ice. Which was exactly why her father had suggested she engage him.

'What *is* your own kind?' she couldn't resist asking.

'The sexy, single and preferably silent type,' he answered.

'You left out beautiful—or isn't that important?'

'It's not my priority. Beautiful women play hard to get, and personally I find chasing them a bore.'

'I thought the chase was all.'

'Perhaps that's because you haven't been caught yet!'

A hot wave of colour swept over her face. There was nothing she could do to stop it, and she knew Rayner had seen it, too, for a faint glint came into his eyes.

'I didn't mean to embarrass you,' he apologised.

'I'm not embarrassed,' she denied. 'I changed colour because I was angry.' She saw from one raised eyebrow that he was waiting for her to explain, and cleverly improvised. 'I may forget you're my chauffeur occasionally, Rayner, but don't *you*.'

She returned to her sun-lounger and opened her book. When she glanced up a moment later his tall, broad-shouldered figure was striding in the direction of the villa.

She ran her tongue over her lips. Rayner had all the attributes to turn a girl's head—even one as level as her own: looks, charm and a devil-may-care attitude that made one long to take him down a peg or two. Yet to contemplate any kind of emotional involvement with him was ludicrous. Given the difference in their status, it could only end in disaster.

Mentally she gave herself a shake. Why was she thinking of him in this fatuous way? A few hours ago she had vowed to make him toe the line and dance to *her* tune. Yet here she was thinking of him as a lover. Talk about crazy! Regardless of how attractive he was, he was a man who had done nothing to utilise his intelligence, preferring to work for a comparative pittance.

So why was she drawn to him? She had always admired successful men, and on that score Mark Rayner was a non-starter.

She sighed. It was impossible to rationalise

emotions. But, like measles, once affected, you
were stuck until the infection wore off!

CHAPTER FOUR

CHARLOTTE was surprised by the way Rayner conducted himself with her friends that evening.

Because she had given him the night off, he wore his own clothes, a grey silk shirt and trousers, and could easily have passed for one of her guests. However, he kept tactfully in the background, though her girlfriends were soon buzzing around him, attracted to his dark good looks like bees to honey. But he rebuffed their advances diplomatically, managing to give the impression that he was doing it with the utmost reluctance.

Annoyingly, Barry Davenport didn't put in an appearance, telephoning before dinner to say his sister had arrived unexpectedly from New York, and he felt obliged to spend the evening with her on the yacht.

'I'll see you in the morning, honey.' He blew a kiss down the receiver. 'Meanwhile, don't go off with any of the competition, will you?'

'Bad news?' Rayner asked as she returned to the terrace, where the dinner-table was set. 'You seem put out.'

'Nothing you need concern yourself with,' she replied shortly, sweeping past him to take her place at the head of the table.

It was past midnight before the party broke up, and

41

as she waved the last of her friends down the driveway
Charlotte looked around for the chauffeur to
compliment him on his behaviour—after all, if she
told him off when she was annoyed with him, he was
entitled to praise when she was pleased. But he was
nowhere to be seen, and, deciding he had assumed she
was safe for the night and had taken himself to bed,
she did the same, falling asleep the moment her head
touched the pillow.

A delicious smell of coffee awakened her, and she
lazily opened her eyes as Maria set a silver tray with
coffee and croissants on the bedside-table. Charlotte's
eyes went instantly to her gold bedside-clock, and she
blinked in surprise as she saw it was ten, for she rarely
slept late.

'I must have had too much wine,' she yawned.

'Or too much dancing,' Maria answered with the
familiarity of five years' service. 'I watched you from
my window and you didn't sit down for a moment.
Who were you trying to impress?'

'No one,' Charlotte replied irritably, for it was
hardly feasible to admit her performance had been for
her chauffeur's benefit! In the cold light of day it
seemed too tawdry to even admit it to herself. 'Mr
Davenport couldn't come, and the other men are
absolute drips.'

'Then why did you invite them?' Maria asked with
Gallic practicality.

'Because they're the best of a boring bunch.'

With a sniff of disapproval, the woman stalked out.

When Charlotte finally went down to the pool,
Barry was there. Twenty-eight, and of average height,

he was attractive in an all-American boy-next-door way: athletic build, square-cut features and streaky blond hair. Heir to a steel fortune, he had more looks than brains, though it had taken her a while to see it, for he disguised his lack of intelligence behind an ability to memorise and quote what others said. If it hadn't been for his father's business association with hers, she would have stopped seeing him long ago.

'Why didn't you bring your sister with you?' she asked after he had greeted her with a kiss. 'Or is she still tired after the flight?'

'Lucy never has jet lag. She's gone shopping in Nice—it's her favourite occupation!'

From the corner of her eye Charlotte spied Mark Rayner sitting behind a mound of bushes on the grassy ridge above the pool area. She waved to let him know she had discovered his hiding-place; then, feeling pleased with herself, she concentrated on Barry.

Mark, well aware why she had waved at him, was amused. Had he really wished to remain hidden, he could easily have done so. But he had wanted her to be aware of him.

Although he doubted whether an attempt would be made to kidnap her in her home or on the estate, he wished to be close at hand, and he made himself more comfortable on the ground, knowing he was in for a long session. It was years since he had done a stake-out, and it was salutary to be reminded of the dangers inherent in this type of work. High-ranking operators in Intelligence sometimes became unmindful of this—to their peril.

'Microphones hidden in the wristwatch and television cameras under the bed may be fine for cinema audiences,' Sir Elrick was fond of saying, 'but the success of an operation more frequently stems from remaining on the job twenty-four hours a day, going over the smallest detail with a fine-tooth comb and never leaving anything to chance.'

Well, I'm certainly obeying his rules, Mark thought. By the time this assignment's over, I'll have counted every hair on Charlotte Beauville's head! He glanced downwards. And lovely hair it was, too. Watch it, Rayner, he warned. Yet it was impossible not to be aware of her beauty as she sprawled on the blue and white mattress, and far too easy to imagine himself in bed with her, her mouth opening beneath his, her legs parting to receive him. He doubted whether she was a virgin—it was years since he had met a girl who was—though she had an untouched air about her, as if she hadn't yet known the passions of experienced lovemaking. Pity they hadn't met under different circumstances. The firm line of his mouth curved. It would have been fun to . . .

Stop it, he warned himself again, knowing it was essential he keep a clear head. And that meant having his emotions under control, not dreaming of ways to excite that full-breasted, slender body. Charlotte Beauville was an assignemnt, and he dared not forget it.

Down by the pool, Charlotte and Barry had come to life and were soon cavorting in the water like playful porpoises. After a while they tired of this and settled on their mattresses until lunch was served. The music was going full blast, but they appeared oblivious to it and chattered away animatedly. Can't be anything worth while with such a racket going on, Mark thought morosely.

For him it was a long, tedious day, and he was delighted when the couple finally gathered their belongings and left the pool.

Charlotte had been constantly aware of Rayner watching her, and as she passed the clump of bushes where he had been hiding she called to him. 'You can come out now, Rayner. You really are a glutton for punishment, sitting there for hours in this heat. Mr Davenport's quite capable of looking after me.'

'I'm used to the heat, miss,' Rayner said, emerging.

'Maybe you are. But it wasn't necessary.' Charlotte turned to Barry. 'This is Mark Rayner, my new chauffeur.'

'Hi, Rayner,' Barry said. 'Miss Beauville's just been informing me what an excellent diver you are. How about a display?'

'I only mentioned it when discussing *your* diving,' Charlotte said hurriedly. 'Rayner isn't a performing dolphin, and this isn't Sea World.'

'It sure isn't,' Barry chuckled, 'it's Future World. It took me ten minutes this morning to get clearance through the front gates. Your computer was on the blink and didn't recognise me.'

'I'm afraid that was my fault,' the chauffeur apologised. 'I pressed the wrong button and things went a little haywire.'

'Who gave you permission to go into the computer-room?' Charlotte asked.

'Your father wanted me to familiarise myself with every aspect of security in the house and grounds.'

'He never mentioned it to me.'

'He only decided when he called this morning.'

'He called this morning?' she echoed, puzzled.

'Yes, to say he was leaving Rome for New York and expected to be away for a week.'

'Why didn't he speak to *me*?' Charlotte demanded.

'You were asleep, and he didn't want to disturb you.'

'Come on, Sharly,' Barry put in impatiently. 'Where's that drink you promised me?'

Shrugging, she continued towards the villa, Rayner bringing up the rear.

'I thought we'd have dinner at the Flamingo tonight,' Barry went on. 'There's a new group playing there who are supposed to be sensational.'

'Sounds lovely.' Charlotte glanced round at her chauffeur. 'Do I have your permission to go?' she enquired sweetly.

'Of course, Miss Beauville. I'll drive you.'

'There's no need. Mr Davenport will.'

'It's your father's orders that I take you wherever you go.'

'Don't get uptight about it,' Barry intervened. 'I know exactly how your father feels. When you have a jewel, you have to guard it.'

'I'm not an object,' Charlotte said crossly. 'I'm

human, remember?'

'How can I forget?'

Barry put an arm around her waist and Rayner turned away, making Charlotte very conscious of the freckled hand on her skin.

'Don't, Barry,' she said, pulling free of him and walking faster. 'Can't you see you're embarrassing Rayner?'

'He'd better get used to it if he's going to follow us around!'

Rayner said nothing, but Charlotte was aware of him remaining on the terrace as she went into the living-room. Despite herself, she was sorry for him. Playing third wheel on a hot day wasn't the most pleasant of jobs.

'Pour a long drink for Rayner as well,' she asked Barry, who was busy at the bar.

'For heaven's sake, Sharly, don't start treating him as a friend.'

'I'll treat him any way I choose.'

'You mean offhand as well as friendly?' Barry muttered. 'You really are the most contrary girl in the world.'

He would have thought her even more so had he been privy to her thoughts as she changed for her dinner date with him. Had it not been for Rayner's patent disapproval of her leaving the estate, she wouldn't have agreed to go. A whole day with Barry was more than enough, without making a night of it, too. But that damned chauffeur had put her back up . . .

Maria came into the room with two freshly

pressed dresses, and Charlotte eyed them critically.

'I don't fancy either of those. I want something more eye-catching.'

Surveying herself later in the mirror, she knew the champagne silk she had selected was the right choice. The soft material clung to every line of her body, outlining her full breasts and prominent nipples, and caressing the rounded curve of her stomach. Its colour was so similar to her tanned skin, it was hard to know where one began and the other ended. She had brushed her hair until it glowed like flame, then swept it to one side of her face, exposing a finely shaped ear dotted with a large, flawless emerald.

Irreverently, she stuck out her tongue at herself, and her eyes, jungle green tonight and fringed by curling dark lashes, smiled back at her.

Kai, the Malaysian butler, was hovering by the front door as she came downstairs, and she smiled at him. 'Is my car waiting?'

He nodded, and she stepped outside. Mark Rayner stood by the bullet-proof black Ferrari, holding the back door open for her. To her surprise he was in chauffeur's uniform, yet she still couldn't think of him as an employee, and she slid into the passenger seat.

Silently he took his place beside her and set the car in motion. The long driveway was floodlit, but occasionally the trees screened the lights, and he drove with the headlamps full on.

He handled the car as fast and competently as Roberts, but there any resemblance between the two men ended. Despite Roberts' thirteen years' service, he had never once stepped out of line. Friendly but respectful, faithful and uncomplaining, he was the perfect family retainer. True, Rayner was more her generation, but this did not account for his bossy attitude and lack of deference, nor for his indefinable air of superiority.

She half swivelled to study him. In profile she was more conscious of the strength of his jawline and his fine-cut mouth. He had a good-shaped head too, and his thick dark hair was well-cut. Even in his uniform he had an unconscious air of style.

'Is your jacket uncomfortable?' she asked, noticing him opening the top button.

'A little.'

'Order yourself another style, then. What's your preference?'

'I'd appreciate a less constricting jacket.'

'In summer, Roberts never wore one during the day, and I'm quite happy for you to do the same.'

'Thank you, miss.'

'You're still "missing" me,' she reprimanded.

'I've hardly had the chance,' he said softly.

Charlotte bit back a smile. 'I can do without the jokes, Rayner. As to your uniform, in the evening you can wear a linen jacket, as long as it isn't white. I don't want you mistaken for my escort.'

'Naturally.'

Resolving not to rise to his subtle baiting, she said conversationally, 'Do you have a girlfriend, Rayner?'

'Not at the moment.'

'But you'll want time off, so let me know when you do. I didn't mean it when I said you were only free at *my* convenience.'

'I realised that, Miss Beauville. You and your father have the reputation for treating your staff considerably.'

'Thank you,' she said, and settled back in her seat, only then noticing they were driving away from Antibes, towards Nice. 'We're collecting Mr Davenport from his yacht in Antibes harbour,' she reminded him.

'I took the liberty of changing the arrangement, Miss Beauville. I thought it safer for you to meet him at the restaurant. The harbour's a very busy area.'

'You think a kidnapper's going to grab me and carry me off on a speedboat?' she asked sarcastically.

'It's a possibility.'

'You've seen too many Bond movies!'

'If you read the papers, you'll know that these days there's little difference between fact and fiction. Don't be angry with me,' he added. 'I'm only thinking of your safety.'

'Do you always apply yourself so conscientiously?'

'Yes.' He pressed his foot hard on the accelerator.

'Not too fast,' she rebuked.

'Does it worry you?'

'Not particularly. But it will do Barry good to wait for me!' She glanced at Rayner. 'I suppose you think me bad-mannered?'

'It's not my concern.'

'But you don't approve of them do you? You don't approve of me.'

'I find you bright and amusing, Miss Beauville.'

'You left out beautiful,' she mocked.

'That goes without saying. You're one of the loveliest girls I've seen.'

He changed gear, his lean fingers inadvertently brushing against her skirt. Intensely aware of it, she tried to keep her voice casual.

'If we'd met as equals, Rayner, would you have asked me for a date?' Hearing herself, she almost laughed—that she, who could have any man she chose, should pose such a question to this man and care about the answer!

'It's safer if I don't reply,' he said.

'I didn't think you were a man who liked to play safe.'

'I'm not—but neither do I enjoy playing with fire.'

'Does that mean you've been burned?' she asked.

'Singed,' he corrected.

'Was it by a woman you worked for?'

'No. I told you, I stick to my own kind. And if you'll forgive my frankness, so should you. If you're tired of Mr Davenport, I'm sure there are plenty of suitable replacements panting in the wings.'

Charlotte knew she had been rebuffed but, knowing she had deserved it, said nothing. She thought of the 'suitable replacements' Rayner had referred to, and stifled a sigh. They were mostly cast in Barry's mould, and she despaired of meeting the man who would fulfil the dreams she cherished, dreams she had never disclosed to anyone.

'I'm afraid you misunderstood my question, Rayner,' she said aloud. 'It was pure curiosity. As a man, you have as much appeal for me as a gorilla!'

In the brightness of an oncoming car's headlights, she saw his mouth firm, and knew she had angered him. But when he spoke his tone was equable.

'It's nice to know where I stand with you, Miss Beauville. Thank you.' He slackened speed and swung into a driveway leading to the sandy-beige façade of an elegant restaurant. 'Le Flamingo,' he announced, bringing the car to a stop.

She saw his hand move under his jacket as he jumped out and came round to open the door for her. Glancing to left and right, he adroitly shielded her with his body as she took the single step necessary to bring her into the foyer.

'I can see you know what you're doing, Rayner. You're a real "minder", aren't you? Not a chauffeur at all.' Staring into his eyes, she saw they were deep pools of fathomless grey, and knew with sudden conviction that he was a man of many secrets. 'Don't bother thinking up a lie,' she snapped. 'I'm no fool.'

'I'm aware of that, Miss Beauville.' Momentarily his lids lowered. 'Call me if you need me. I won't be far away.'

'You never are,' she said waspishly, and walked towards Barry's welcoming smile.

CHAPTER FIVE

CHARLOTTE regarded Barry across the table and stifled a yawn. The evening was barely half-way through and was already a bore. She glanced surreptitiously at her watch, wondering how soon she could decently suggest they leave.

What was Rayner doing? She had been angry when she had left him, and so had omitted to tell him that whenever his duties coincided with mealtimes he was at liberty to get himself something to eat and charge it to her. She smiled to herself. Perhaps it was as well she hadn't. He would probably have reserved a table here, right next to her!

She eyed her watch again, and then Barry. He had drunk more than usual tonight and his fair skin was flushed.

'It's late,' she murmured. 'I want to go home.'

'Don't be silly, Sharly, the night's just beginning. I thought we'd go on somewhere and dance. There's a new club in St Tropez——'

'Sorry, Barry, I'd rather not. I'm too tired to drive that far.'

'You won't be driving, sweetheart. I will.'

'I have my car and chauffeur here,' she reminded him.

'Send him home. I'm perfectly capable of driving

you.'

'No, you're not. You're drunk.'

Barry looked pained. 'I've only had a bottle of wine. I can take twice that much and not feel the effect. I'm used to it.'

'Proud of it, too,' she said drily.

'Well, I'm not ashamed.' He wagged a finger at her. 'Anyway, what's it to you? You're acting like a nagging wife. Hey, that's a great idea. Why don't we make it for real? You'd make me the happiest guy in the world if you said yes.'

'I'm afraid not.' She forced a smile to soften the words. 'I'm fond of you, Barry, but not enough to marry you.'

'Do you think I'm after your money?' His voice rose, making the head waiter move discreetly closer. 'I may not have as much as you—heck, who has?—but I've enough not to need yours.'

'I know,' she soothed. 'And that isn't why I said no. It's because I don't love you.'

'Why not?' he demanded, made aggressive by alcohol. 'Plenty of other girls do. Only *you* play hard to get.'

'I'm not playing. I *am* hard to get—and impossible as far as you're concerned!' Pushing back her chair, she rose and stalked off, nodding imperceptibly to the head waiter, who instantly stepped into Barry's path as he tried to follow her.

'You haven't paid your bill, sir,' he said quietly.

'You know who I am. Send it to the yacht.'

'I'm sorry, sir . . .'

Not waiting to hear more, Charlotte fled. Only as

she emerged from the restaurant did she wonder what to do if her car wasn't there. But in that moment Rayner was beside her.

'Anything wrong, Miss Beauville?'

'Yes—no. I just want to leave.'

Shielding her as before, he escorted her to the Ferrari and, without asking, held the front door open and waited for her to slide into the passenger seat.

Absorbed in her thoughts—mainly concerning Barry and whether she had been too harsh—Charlotte did not speak until they were bowling along the coast road.

'Thank goodness you were waiting for me, Rayner. I'd have had a fit if Barry had come out and found me there.'

'I was outside the whole evening.'

'What about your meal?'

'I'm used to long hours without food.'

'You'll give yourself an ulcer—or so my father's always telling me. Let's stop and get you a sandwich.'

'There's no need. I'm sure I can make it back without collapsing.'

The amusement in his voice annoyed her. Here she was, being considerate, and he was making fun of her again.

'Well, if you're not hungry, *I* am.'

'Didn't you enjoy your dinner?' He sounded surprised.

'Not much. Mr Davenport had too much to drink, and I got bored and lost my appetite.'

'I see.'

There was silence, and Charlotte knew he was

debating whether to say what he wanted to.

'Go on, Rayner. What's on your mind?'

He flung her a grin. 'As you seem able to read it, *you* tell me.'

'My powers of deduction only go so far!' she smiled back. 'Come on, out with it.'

'I was wondering if you're often bored with your dates.'

'Too often,' she admitted.

'Have you thought of widening your circle of friends?'

'Frequently. But it's not easy when you're born and bred into an exclusive clique.' Leaning back in her seat, she rested her head against the soft, white leather. 'How *does* one break out of it?'

'Ever considered taking a job? You've an art degree and——'

'I'm too used to giving orders to take them!'

'I was thinking more in terms of opening your own gallery. Turning your hobby into a business, as it were.'

'In theory it's a good idea, but in practice the people who'd patronise me are the ones I want to get away from! No, one can't run from one's destiny, and mine is the Beauville money. I'm stuck with it.'

Resting her head against the back of the seat, she studied the man at the wheel. He had taken off his jacket and she was conscious of the ripple of muscles beneath his shirt. Strangely, she was even more physically aware of him at this moment than seeing him half naked by the pool.

'That's why my father's so fussy about whom I

date,' she went on. 'He's hoping I'll marry a man capable of eventually stepping into his shoes.'

'They won't be easy to fill.'

'Too right. None of the men I know has one tenth of his ability.'

'You're only twenty-three, Miss Beauville. There's plenty of time to meet the right person.'

'The problem is that he might value his independence—like you, Rayner. Didn't you once say *you'd* never marry a woman with money?'

'The right man wouldn't be marrying you because of your money, but in spite of it,' he stated flatly.

'Ah, the "right man",' she echoed. 'But where is he?'

'Somewhere out there.' Rayner waved an arm. 'Keep on looking.'

The lights of Antibes glittered ahead of them, and Charlotte sat up straight. 'Let's stop in town for a snack. The Place de Gaulle is empty at this hour, and we can park the car and take a stroll.'

Rayner's answer was to increase speed, and not slacken it until they had left the Place de Gaulle far behind. Charlotte sat up straight. Drat the man! Give him an inch and he took a mile!

'Rayner, stop!'

'I'd be happier if we went somewhere else, Miss Beauville.'

'Why?'

'Antibes is too quiet at night. I'd prefer Juan-les-Pins.'

She thought of Juan, with its noise and bustle. It

wasn't her scene, and she was disappointed it was his.

'It's safer to be where there are people,' he explained.

'You said the opposite when we were supposed to collect Barry from the harbour,' she argued. 'What's the difference?'

'Accessibility and escape routes.'

'You're becoming as paranoid as my father,' she flung at him. 'There are loads of potential prey besides myself. This stretch of coastline is crawling with Arab princesses, movie stars, and plain, ordinary Texan billionaires! So why on earth should anyone kidnap *me*?'

'Because it's a well-publicised fact that your father idolises you, and would pay anything to get you back.'

'He's not unique in that respect. Any father—or husband, for that matter—would do the same.' She placed a hand on the gear lever. 'Go back to Antibes, Rayner. Juan's awful in high season.'

'It's Juan or the villa.'

'Then it's the villa,' she snapped. 'And what's more, you can pack your bags in the morning and leave.'

The car slowed and Rayner glanced at her. 'I'm only concerned for your safety, Miss Beauville, and I'd be pleased if you didn't construe my behaviour as rudeness.'

'Are you apologising?' She saw his fingers tighten on the wheel, and waited expectantly for his reply.

'Yes.'

'Then we'll go to Juan,' she conceded. 'There's a fun place on the corner near the casino where they make great sandwiches.'

He sighed. 'I've never met anyone who changes their moods so fast.'

'It's a trait I inherited from my mother,' Charlotte confessed. 'She was Irish.'

'That explains a lot!'

'Meaning?'

'That you annoy, irritate and often infuriate, but you're never boring.'

Charlotte warmed with pleasure. Strange how half-praise from his man gave her more satisfaction that adulation from any other. 'Sounds as if you're paying me a compliment, Rayner.'

'You seem surprised.'

'Well, you don't exactly dole them out to me.'

'It's not my place to.'

'It's not "your place" to countermand my orders, either,' she retorted, 'but it doesn't stop you. I get the impression you use a compliment when it suits you.'

'We all do what suits us,' he said, meaningfully.

Approaching a roundabout, he glanced in the rear-view mirror, as he had frequently done all the way. Charlotte also looked round, but there was no car in sight. This did not last long, for Juan itself was packed, and parking impossible. Only by tipping the casino's attendant, who knew her, were they able to find a place.

'No need to wear your cap and jacket,' she said

quickly, as Rayner stepped from the car.

'I'm afraid the jacket's necessary.' His hand touched the almost imperceptible bulge near the top pocket, which she knew to be his gun.

Trying not to think of it, she strolled beside him to the large, brightly lit café in the centre of the little town. The street was crowded with tourists of every nationality and, though it was past ten, pavement restaurants were packed with diners having late-night meals—lobsters with garlic sauce, fish soup with mussels and prawns, and wooden bowls piled high with fresh green salads.

Charlotte breathed in the aromas and, enjoying the festive mood, revelled in the sense of freedom, of being like everyone else. Yet not quite the same as everyone else, for Rayner was beside her, vigilant, tense, as he tried to hurry her along.

They reached the brightly lit café, where every table—inside as well as out—appeared to be occupied. After a brief exchange of words with one of the waiters, during which she glimpsed a fifty-franc note exchange hands, Rayner turned back to her.

'We'll only have to wait a few seconds.'

'I'm in no hurry. It wasn't necessary to waste your money tipping the waiter.'

'Don't worry about it,' he said coolly. 'Your father allows me an expense account.'

She caught her breath. Arrogant swine! From beneath her lashes she gave him a sidelong glance. He was so damnably attractive, it was increasingly difficult to think of him only as her 'minder'. Yet she must. To enter into a relationship with him would be dangerous and stupid.

The light touch of his hand on her elbow interrupted her reverie.

'Our table's ready,' he said.

Tossing back her hair, she followed the waiter to one by the window, and as she sat down she felt her soft cashmere stole being slipped across her shoulders.

'You might get cold,' Rayner murmured, taking the chair opposite and indicating the electric fan above them.

'Thanks.' She scanned the menu. 'What are you having?'

'A large coffee and a *croque monsieur*. Make it two,' he corrected, as the waiter jotted it down. 'I'm hungrier than I thought. What about you, Miss Beauville?' A gleam of humour lightened his grey eyes. 'Supper will be *my* treat.'

'How terribly sweet of you. Are you sure you can afford it?'

'Providing you don't order caviare!'

'Don't worry. I'll have the same as you.'

The smile he gave her was unexpectedly warm, and they waited for their food in companionable silence, gazing at the crowded pavements through the window and listening to snatches of conversation around them. When their order finally arrived, they tucked into the toasted cheese and ham sandwiches with gusto.

'Why is it that even something as simple as this tastes better when the French make it?' he asked between mouthfuls.

As Charlotte began to reply, a red sports car drew to a stop outside. A laughing crowd tumbled from it, and her heart sank as a dark-haired girl waved to her, then weaved through the tables towards them;

'Hi, Sharly,' she drawled, bright brown eyes darting from her to the man opposite. 'I thought you were having dinner with Barry?'

'I did.' Charlotte's tone closed the subject, and the girl's eyes flickered momentarily to Rayner.

'Aren't you going to introduce me to your friend?'

An imp of mischief took hold of Charlotte, but, about to say he was her new boyfriend, she caught his frigid expression. 'This is Rayner,' she capitulated. 'My new chauffeur.'

'Let me know if you decide he's not right for you,' the girl said throatily. 'I'm looking for a chauffeur, too.'

Charlotte glanced at Rayner, wondering if he was annoyed at being spoken of as if he weren't there. But his expression was aloof.

The girl held out her hand. 'I'd better introduce myself, since Sharly seems reluctant. I'm Lila Bergdorf.'

'How do you do, miss?'

Rayner didn't have a cap to doff, but Charlotte was irritated he had made himself sound so servile. 'I thought you came over to see *me*,' she interposed coldly. 'I didn't realise it was my chauffeur you were interested in.'

Ignoring the comment, Lila directed a wide smile at him. 'Where are you from?'

'England.'

'My favourite country—after the States. I lived in London when my father was at the Embassy.'

'Your friends are waiting for you,' Charlotte cut in.

'Trying to get rid of me?' Lila pouted.

'Clever of you to guess!'

'I didn't realise this was a tête-à-tête.' Lila deliberately leaned towards the chauffeur, so that her breasts, high and full, almost spilled out of her bodice. But Rayner appeared unaware of it, and rose respectfully, waiting for her to leave.

Unembarrassed, she straightened and said huskily, 'I'll be seeing you.' The words were clearly directed at him, though she was looking at Charlotte, who watched sourly as the dark-haired girl sauntered back to her friends.

Rayner sat down. 'Another coffee, Miss Beauville?'

'No, thanks.' All pleasure had gone from the evening, and Charlotte wanted it to end. She was discomfited at being discovered here with Rayner. Lila was a terrible gossip and would be on the phone to everyone first thing tomorrow.

With a weary gesture, she pushed her hair back from her forehead. Her shawl slipped to the ground, and as they both bent to retrieve it their fingers touched. It was as if an electric current ran up her arm, and she drew back sharply and hurried from the café.

Only when they were heading towards the villa did she speak. 'Miss Bergdorf's a man-eater, Rayner. I think it's only fair to warn you.'

'Thank you, miss. I *had* noticed!'

'She'll probably ask you out,' Charlotte continued. 'If you want to accept, you're at liberty to do so.'

'Why the change of heart? Last night you warned me not to "chat up" your girlfriends.'

'Because they were in my home. But I've no business dictating how or with whom you spend your free time.'

The man's mouth curved upwards. 'I've no intention of spending it with Miss Bergdorf. I've better things to do than play lap-dog to bored little rich girls.'

'You're doing that with me.'

'You're my bread and butter—if you'll forgive me saying so—not my jam.'

Her head tilted sharply. 'You're being impossible again! As soon as I treat you as a friend, you're rude.'

'Don't you mean as soon as I say anything you don't like, you wish I'd remember my place?' he countered, and, lifting his foot from the accelerator, the car almost came to a stop. 'You can't have it both ways.'

'I'm aware of that, but . . .' How to explain that the emotions he aroused in her were so puzzling, she couldn't understand them herself?

'Yes?' he prompted.

'Let's forget it.'

'I don't think we can, Miss Beauville. It might happen again.'

'Then it will be better if you left.'

This time he did stop the car—pulling into the kerb and switching off the engine.

'You're attracted to me,' he said tersely. 'That's why you want me to go.'

'How dare you?'

'I dare because my job's at stake. A well-paid job which I don't want to lose.'

'I'll give you severance pay,' she hit back.

'I don't accept money for work I don't do.' He paused. 'Nor do I ever have an affair with an employer. But if you insist, I'll make an exception in your case.'

She assumed he was joking until she saw the sneer on his face. He meant it! For the briefest instant she wondered how it would feel if he kissed her, caressed her, ran his hands over her body.

Yet, if she let him, she would despise herself tomorrow. Her innermost beliefs were too deeply entrenched to pretend that a purely physical relationship would satisfy her. She wanted more than Rayner was capable of giving. He was hard, callous and he clearly despised her.

'If you can't make up your mind, Miss Beauville, perhaps this will help,' he said, and, sliding across the seat, savagely claimed her lips.

There was no tenderness in his touch, only a determination to master her. She beat at his chest but he was too strong for her, and he pushed her back against the door, making it impossible for her to move. Only then did the savagery leave his mouth, and his lips grew gentle as they rubbed against hers—so gentle that she found herself relaxing. As she did, his tongue slid softly into her mouth, rubbing over her own in teasing movements. She whimpered a protest, but this merely served to give him greater entry, and with casual disregard of her cry his tongue explored her more deeply.

Many men had tried to kiss her this way, and occasionally she had allowed them to, but none had shown this man's confidence or sensuality, and certainly none had drawn such a response from her. Her arms stole around his neck and she pressed her body against his, feeling him shudder as her soft breasts were crushed upon the hardness of his chest.

Muttering deep in his throat, he moulded her closer still, his hand sliding behind her to unfasten her dress and expose her creamy, firm breasts, the pointed, rose-pink nipples resembling the sweet-scented buds that clustered against the walls of the villa.

Lowering his head, his lips curved around them. At the touch of his tongue they stiffened, and he drew them deeper into his mouth, sucking on them so fiercely that she cried out with pleasurable agony. Never had she experienced such a wild desire. It flamed through her, linking her throbbing nipples to the throbbing ache between her legs that only he could satisfy.

'You're so beautiful,' he whispered thickly,

raising his head to find her mouth.

Her heart pounded and her emotions spiralled out of control as his hands moved along her back to span her waist before going further down. She was racked by a desire so intense that she felt she was drowning in a depth of emotion she had never known she possessed, experiencing sensations she had never dreamed existed. His hands moved lower, firm upon the softness of her stomach, then lower still to the raging fire between her legs. Her body arched upon his, and feeling his arousal, hard and hot upon her thigh, she took fright, scared of her vulnerability, of giving herself to a man who saw her only as a well-paid job he didn't want to lose.

The knowledge froze all passion, replaced by shame that she had allowed him to hold her, fondle her, lust after her.

'Let me go!' she cried, hitting out at him violently.

He released her at once. 'Don't worry. I've no intention of forcing myself on you.'

The steadiness of his tone stunned her. How could he show such control when only moments ago he had been devoid of it? If only it were possible to contain her own feelings as easily! She was still trembling from his touch, her skin tingling from the feel of his mouth and hands.

Furiously she zipped up her dress, the steel cold against the hot dampness of her back. 'How dare you touch me? Do you think you're so irresistible that I can forget who you are?' Sickened that she had allowed him to see the power he had exerted over her, she wanted to humiliate him as *she* had been humiliated. 'You're a nothing . . . a nobody!'

If she had hoped for a reaction to her insult, she was disappointed, for the silver-grey eyes were as impenetrable as a mountain mist.

'You appeared to be giving it serious thought,' he commented drily.

'I couldn't escape you!'

'You didn't try very hard—until a second ago. Come off it, *Sharly darling*!'

'Why, you . . .' She lunged at him, but he caught her hands in a grip of iron and brought them easily down to her lap.

'Don't you care for the truth?' he jeered. 'From the first morning you've been baiting me, so what did you expect me to do? Take it lying down when I could have *you* lying down?'

He was right, of course, but she would die before admitting it. 'Don't you know when you're being teased, Rayner? Where's your sense of humour?'

'You're a tease all right, Miss Beauville. As for my sense of humour, I don't have any when my job's at stake. Or do you enjoy having a man beg for his livelihood?'

'That's hitting below the belt!' she snapped.

'An appropriate simile—as it's the only part of me that interests you!' He laughed as he saw her discomfiture. 'Sorry if my crudeness offends, but it will take more than a rebuff from you to fool me.'

'You're so conceited and arrogant, nobody

could fool you,' she said furiously. 'You think you know everything about me.'

'I do!' His voice had a rasp to it. 'And frankly, there isn't much I like!'

With a sudden movement he switched on the ignition and pressed his foot so hard on the accelerator that the car shot forward, tyres screeching as they hit a curve on two wheels, and hurled towards the Cap.

CHAPTER SIX

CHARLOTTE stirred restlessly in her sleep, disturbed by her dreams. She flung out an arm and her knuckles hit the bedside-table. With a gasp she awoke, and for a moment lay motionless. Then, as she became fully conscious, she stretched and yawned, her body supple as a kitten. Turning her head on the pillow, she stared at the window. Billowing swathes of silk diffused the bright sunlight, softening the glare. Another lovely day, but she wasn't particularly looking forward to it. After last night, the thought of seeing Rayner made her distinctly uncomfortable.

There was no sign of him when she came down the sweeping staircase half an hour later, nor when she went on to the terrace. The garden was sunny and peaceful, the air fragrant, with two gardeners weeding flowerbeds.

She stood for a while, enjoying the tranquil scene, then went down to the pool. As she approached, she saw Rayner swimming across it with leisurely strokes. She stopped and watched him as he turned to float on his back, his eyes closed against the sun's glare.

Quietly she settled herself on a sun-lounger. But he had heard her and, rolling on to his stomach, he reached the side in a few swift strokes and heaved himself out of the water. Droplets glistened on his

71

skin, emphasising its natural sheen, and brief black swimming-trunks barely covered narrow hips and flat stomach.

'Good morning, Miss Beauville.' He came to stand in front of her.

'Good morning,' she replied, glad dark glasses hid the shadows under her eyes.

There were none under his, and waspishly she decided that sexual frustration had little effect on him. Either that, or he was getting satisfaction elsewhere, and one rejection didn't bother him. Drat the man! He was behaving as if nothing had happened between them last night.

'Why weren't you on the terrace when I came down?' she asked coolly, playing him at his own game.

'You're quite safe in the grounds. They're well-guarded.'

She glanced at the sky. 'A helicopter might swoop down and snatch me away!'

'Impossible. The noise would warn us, and we'd get you to safety in plenty of time.'

'I assume your skills have been put to the test?' she enquired sweetly.

'On the odd occasion.'

'For instance?'

'It wasn't much,' he said offhandedly. 'I was driving down a country road and three policemen had set up a road block ahead of me. Luckily I recognised one of them as a smuggler I'd once encountered.'

'What did you do?'

'Nodded as though I were going to stop, then

accelerated like hell and drove straight through the barricade.'

'Was that when you were with Sir Elrick?' Charlotte leaned forward, the better to see his expression.

Rayner's grey eyes crinkled at the corners. 'Come now, Miss Beauville, you don't expect me to answer you. Discretion is part of my service.'

'I'm glad you're so loyal.' She switched on the radio and lay back. It was news time, none of it good, and mostly concerned with the uprising in Teleguay. Irritably, she flicked it off.

'Aren't you interested in what's going on there?' Rayner asked.

Taken aback that he should question her, she sat up again. 'Why should I be?'

'Your father has big mining interests there.'

'If we lose it all, we'd still be as rich as Croesus,' Her lips pursed. 'Do you think the rebels will win?'

'It's on the cards, yes.' He squinted at her in the sunlight. 'Ever been there?'

'Twice. But only for a short while, so I don't know it well. But the wealth is held by less than one per cent of the population, so I guess I'd give my vote to the rebels.'

'Except they won't be asking for anyone's vote,' he said drily. 'The ballot-box is a dirty word with dictatorships.'

She rested on her side, propping herself on one elbow. 'Are you interested in politics, Rayner?'

'As much as any man in the street.'

'Except you're not "any man", are you?' she

pounced. 'You're brighter and more intelligent that the average. You might even *be* in Intelligence. You've got the right qualities for a spy.'

'Which are?' He grinned.

'Control, perception, quick wit, toughness. Do you want me to go on?'

'If it amuses you.'

'Oh, it does, very much.' Charlotte was enjoying herself. 'Tell me, do you have a radio transmitter in your ear and a micro-camera in your watch?'

'Clever of you to guess.' He raised his wrist to show the digital Rolex clasping it. 'When you see me do this,' he tapped his fingers lightly on the glass face, 'I'm sending out a lethal dose of nerve gas! I have other tricks, too, but I'm not going to give them away.'

'You should have used nerve gas last night.' It was out before she could stop herself, and she cursed her runaway tongue.

'I prefer my women sensuous, not senseless,' Rayner said coolly.

'A woman would *have* to be senseless to give herself to you!' she said dulcetly.

'To each his own.'

'You've never said a truer word, Rayner. You'd do well to remember it.'

His jaw clenched, and she was delighted her thrust had hit home. Yet deep down she deplored the snobbishness of her remark. In this day and age, what you made of yourself was more important than what social strata you came from. Heavens, her mother's parents had been farmers, and her father's shopkeepers.

'You have a visitor,' Rayner warned, glancing over her shoulder, and Charlotte tilted her head to see Lila approaching.

'Not me,' she said. 'You're the one she's come to see!'

'Then she's wasting her time.'

'So you intimated last night. But this is today, and not many men can withstand a frontal assault from Lila.'

'Even a *full* frontal wouldn't tempt me!' he asserted.

Though amused by his answer, Charlotte was sceptical as to its truth. 'She might grow on you.'

'I suppose she must have something if she's a friend of yours.'

'She isn't,' Charlotte replied. 'We have lots of mutual friends and are always running into each other.'

She watched Lila draw near. Her sultry beauty, boldly advertised in last night's low-cut dress, was proclaimed even more obviously today. Two wisps of white barely covered her breasts and the rounded curve of her pubic bone, and as she paused beside Rayner she carelessly brushed against him, her breasts pressing against his arm. But neither by gesture nor expression did he indicate awareness of it.

'Hi.' She smiled, glancing from one to the other. 'I hope I'm not interrupting anything?'

'As it happens, you are.' A mischievous glint made Charlotte's eyes shamrock green. 'Rayner was expounding his views on sex and the single girl,' she lied.

'Really?' Lila's eyebrows rose. 'What are they?'

'Decidedly old-fashioned!' Charlotte said meaningfully.

But sarcasm was lost on Lila. 'Perhaps I can change them.' She gave him the full battery of her eyes. 'I can be very persuasive.'

'I'm sure you can, Miss Bergdorf.' Rayner spoke for the first time.

'Lila, please,' she corrected with a half-smile. 'But I don't know your first name, and Rayner's too formal.'

'Not for Miss Beauville,' he said pointedly.

'But I'm not Miss Beauville.' Scarlet-tipped fingers touched his powerful biceps. 'So what is it?'

'Mark Alexander.'

'Hmm, nice.'

'Let's hope he doesn't act like an Alexander,' Charlotte said. 'He came to an untimely end at about the same age Rayner is now!'

'But he left his mark,' Lila said softly, her eyes speaking to him of other thoughts. 'Will *you*?'

'I try to give good service, Miss Bergdorf.'

'I bet you do.' She glanced at the pool. 'Are you a good swimmer?'

'It isn't for me to say, miss.'

'Rayner excels at every sport,' Charlotte intervened.

'Lucky you.' Lila smiled.

'Stop being obvious, Lila.'

'Am I embarrassing you, Rayner?' the girl enquired.

'No, miss. I'm used to dealing with all sorts of

peculiar situations.'

There was a momentary silence before Lila laughed. 'Let's have a swim, Mark. I'll race you.'

'I have to clean the car, Miss Bergdorf.'

'I'm sure it can wait. And I thought we agreed you'd call me Lila.'

'*You* agreed,' he corrected politely. 'Whether I do or not depends on Miss Beauville.'

'You don't mind, do you, Sharly?' Lila mocked.

Irritated that Rayner had put her on the spot, Charlotte shrugged. 'I don't own my chauffeur. I only employ him.'

She lay back and closed her eyes, waiting for Mark—how easy it was to think of him that way—to reiterate that he had to clean the car. Instead she heard a splash, and raising her head saw the two figures cleaving through the water. Except her eyes focused on only one: the powerful body of the man. No wonder Lila was pursuing him. Other than money—and Lila had more than enough for the two of them—he had everything a girl could want: looks, brains and a cool detachment that added to his sensuous attraction. One was aware of the icy control he was putting on himself, and she doubted if there was a woman alive who wouldn't feel the urge to break it down, to discover the primitive, passionate man beneath, as she had done last night.

'You're really missing something,' Lila called. 'The temperature's perfect.'

Which is more than I can say for mine, Charlotte thought mutinously. It rises every time Mark

Rayner comes near me.

'I don't feel energetic enough for a swim,' she called back. 'I think I'll have a coffee. Care for a cup?'

'Love one, darling. And some fruit, too. I skipped breakfast and I'm famished.'

'Anything for you, Rayner?' Charlotte enquired.

'A pineapple juice, please.'

Picking up the house phone, she gave the order, watching from the corner of her eye as Rayner emerged from the pool. He stood on the edge, skin glistening brown, hair almost black now it was wet, and put out a needless hand to help Lila climb out via the steps. The two bodies were both tanned magnificent bronze, as if cast in the same mould, and Charlotte wondered if he was as immune to Lila's charms as he averred.

The girl settled on a lounger next to him and, reaching into her bag, extracted a bottle of suntan lotion. 'Be an angel and rub some on my back.' She held out the bottle to Mark. 'I've a strained shoulder muscle.'

'And you can manage to swim?' Charlotte put in sweetly.

'Strange, isn't it?' Lila was unabashed, and Charlotte turned away, ostensibly to rummage for a tissue, in reality resenting the sight of Mark Rayner's hands on Lila's body.

'Do you work, Miss Berg—Lila?' Mark enquired conversationally as she finished a slice of melon.

'You mean like Sharly?' Lila saw the lift of his

eyebrows. 'Don't you know she's head of the Beauville Foundation?'

'I'd no idea.'

Lila made a face at Charlotte. 'Why the secrecy, darling?'

'It's no secret. But there's nothing to tell.'

'You're too modest.' Lila wiped her fingers on a napkin, then gave her attention to Mark. 'Miss Beauville travels to the remotest and poorest parts of the world to check how the funds are being utilised. A bit like your Princess Anne.'

'Don't exaggerate,' Charlotte protested.

'I'm not. You work terribly hard.'

'Nonsense. I get red carpet treatment wherever I go, so you can hardly say I suffer.'

'Red carpet in the jungle and desert? Why, darling, I doubt if they even have rush matting! You do a great job and should get credit for it.'

'I don't want credit—or publicity. How did you hear about it, anyway?'

'From one of the security men who went with you on your last trip. In a relaxed moment he let it drop.'

Knowing Lila's penchant for husky young men, there was no prize for guessing what he had been relaxing from.

'Sorry if I spoke out of turn,' Lila added. 'I assumed Mark already knew, as he's working for you.'

'Was there any reason why you didn't mention it, Miss Beauville?' Rayner asked when Lila disappeared to 'powder her nose' a few moments later. 'Why did you make out you lead a lotus life?'

'Because talking about it belittles what I do,' she answered truthfully.

'I see.'

His tone showed that he did, that he saw many things about her others didn't. She rested her eyes on him. In his bathing-trunks it was impossible to guess his occupation. Dressed, he was every inch the chauffeur, as he would be every inch the soldier or doctor, if that was the role he was asked to play. Only undressed would one see anything of the real Mark Rayner.

A tall, lean man with a narrow, contained face that gave away nothing of his thoughts. A loner who, for money, laid his life on the line to save someone else's. Unexpectedly she visualised him lying dead on the ground at her feet, his life lost in an effort to save hers. Anguish stabbed her. What a waste it would be. She blinked rapidly, then found him bending over her.

'Don't you feel well? You're very pale.'

'I'm fine,' she whispered. 'I——'

'Anyone for tennis?' Lila called, sauntering back in a loose cotton top that skimmed her thighs, and directing her gaze at Mark.

Over her head, his eyes met Charlotte's. 'Will you be playing too, Miss Beauville?'

'And inhibit your game? No, Rayner, I'm happy to stay here.'

As the two of them walked off, Charlotte poured herself another coffee. Soon the slap of tennis balls on rackets punctuated the silence, and every now and then Lila's laugh rang out.

Reaching for the radio beside her, Charlotte switched it on, refusing to question why she should want to drown out the sound, why it should so disturb her.

CHAPTER SEVEN

LILA was a regular visitor in the days that followed, and made no pretence that it was to see Charlotte. Mark Rayner continued to appear disinterested, though whether from circumspection or genuine immunity Charlotte could not decide. Somehow she thought the latter, for, had he succumbed, Lila would unquestionably have boasted about it.

Charlotte's father returned at the weekend, and much to her annoyance spent several hours closeted with him in his study.

'I hear you've stopped seeing Barry,' he commented when he joined her on the terrace later that Saturday afternoon. 'Any particular reason?'

She frowned, guessing Mark must have told him. 'He bores me, and drinks too much.'

Charles Beauville sighed. 'You know him best, I suppose, but he struck me as a pleasant young man.'

'Is that how Rayner strikes you, too?' Charlotte asked casually. 'You seem to have taken quite a shine to him.'

'Does that mean *you* haven't?'

'He's all right. But to be honest, I can't decide about him.'

'Lila doesn't appear to have that problem.'

'Did Rayner discuss her with you?' Charlotte was

surprised.

'Not exactly. She called him on the intercom while we were talking—insisted on speaking to him—and said she was down by the pool.' He smiled. 'She's always had a penchant for good-looking young men.'

'Rayner has more than looks.' Unexpectedly, Charlotte found herself defending him. 'He's bright—too bright for the job, and I was wondering if——'

'I had another position for him?' her father finished for her. 'Probably, but he's happy in his job, which is more than many of us can say.'

'A sloth is happy, too. But there's more to life than idling it away. That's why Rayner annoys me,' she said. 'He's content to waste his abilities.'

Thick grey eyebrows rose. 'Watch your step, my dear. Mark isn't the kind of man you can take over—or make over.'

'Mark?' she echoed. 'It's unlike you to be on first-name terms.'

'He prefers me to call him Mark,' came the gruff reply.

'He's never asked *me* to.'

'Because he works directly for you, and to tell you what he prefers would be an impertinence.'

'That wouldn't stop him. He isn't a retiring violet when it comes to voicing his opinions! Anyway, I don't employ him, *you* do, and I'm fed up with not being allowed to live my life as I choose.'

'Don't let's go into that again! I want what's best for you, and your safety is my prime concern.' His features softened—he was never able to sustain anger with her for long. 'Find yourself a husband, my dear, then you can argue with him as to how to protect yourself.'

Head to one side, she pondered on his comment. 'Would you object if I married someone who didn't want to go into Beauville Industries?'

'Not at all. Though it means that when I die or retire, the company will be run by a faceless board of directors—unless one of my grandchildren shows an aptitude for commerce!'

Charlotte laughed and caught his hand. 'I wish I had a head for business. I often feel I've let you down.'

'What nonsense. You're my daughter and I love you—even though you can't add two and two!' Ruffling her hair, he rose. 'I'm going inside to study a few documents.'

Alone on the terrace, Charlotte leaned back against the floral cushions and closed her eyes, debating whether to go to the pool or take a stroll in the grounds. Neither appealed. It was too hot to walk, and she was in no mood to chat to Lila.

A rivulet of perspiration ran down her temple and she raised her hand to wipe it away. It was caught in a strong grasp and, startled, she opened her eyes to see laughing blue ones peering down at her.

'Johnny! What a fright you gave me.'

'Sorry—I wanted to surprise you.'

'You certainly did. When did you arrive?'

'We docked at six this morning.' Johnny Craxton's hobby was competitive sailing, and he was never far from his boat.

Charlotte had known him for years and

occasionally toyed with the idea of marrying him. But, apart from the fact that she didn't love him, she had no desire to play second fiddle to the sea or the polo field—to both of which he was devoted. Cowes week always felt like a month to her, and a day at Hurlingham an eternity! Hardly a recipe for a successful marriage. She would also be exchanging one gilded cage for another, for Johnny would cosset and protect her as much as her father.

He sat beside her—an attractive man with light brown hair and neat features. He had the typical upper-class Englishman's attitude to clothes, regarding them simply as covering. When Charlotte had stayed with him at his home, he had been positively shabby in baggy corduroys and a hand-knitted sweater with holes at the elbows, patched with leather.

Today he was reasonably presentable in an open-neck white shirt and shorts that showed his slim physique to advantage. All the same, no one would have guessed him to be heir to one of the oldest and richest titles in England.

'How long are you here for?' she asked.

'A week. Then I'm racing at Cowes. I was hoping you'd join me.'

'I hate sailing.'

'Just come and be decorative.'

'That's what you said last year, and I ended up scrubbing the deck!'

'But you enjoyed it.'

'It was a change,' she admitted. 'I'd never used a

scrubbing brush before.'

'Marry me and you can use one the whole time!' he teased.

Laughing, she rose and linked her arm through his. 'Let's go to the pool. I fancy a swim.'

Together they strolled over the lawn and down the steps. 'Who's the chap playing tennis with Lila?' Johnny asked.

'My new chauffeur cum "minder".'

'You must miss Roberts.'

'I do. But this one's working out quite well.'

'Especially with Lila!' Johnny commented. 'He's exactly the type she goes for.'

'He's as much a gentleman as you are,' Charlotte rejoined.

'Don't tell me you're smitten too?' Johnny said wryly.

'Because I judge him by what he is rather than where he comes from?'

'Hey, I'm no snob. But I can't see any of us having much in common with him.'

With an effort, Charlotte controlled her temper. 'He's very intelligent. You'll see for yourself when you meet him.'

'I can't wait.'

As if on cue, Mark and Lila appeared. She was breathless but unquestionably delighted with herself, and Charlotte wondered whether it was because she had played well, or was making progress in another game.

'He beat me hollow,' Lila announced. 'But he showed me how to improve my backhand.' Dark eyes rested on him. 'You're good enough to be a professional coach.'

'Thanks.' He smiled, then glanced at the man facing him.

Charlotte knew he was waiting to be introduced, and perversely didn't, angry when Lila took over.

'Mark, this is Lord Craxton. If you know anything about sailing, you'll have heard of him.'

'I have, indeed. Pleased to meet you, m'lord.'

Johnny nodded. 'We must have a game some time soon. I think I'll be more of a match for you than Lila.'

How cosy, Charlotte thought irritably. Everyone on first-name terms except me. But she had no intention of joining the club.

'I'm going for a swim,' she stated. 'Coming, Johnny?' Pointedly she ignored the other two and slid into the water, allowing it to lap soothingly against her. There was a splash behind her, and instinctively she knew it was Rayner.

'Have I done anything to annoy you?' he asked, drawing level with her.

'What makes you ask?'

'You don't exactly hide your feelings.'

'Unlike you!'

'Would you rather I told Lila I can't stand her?'

'Certainly not.'

'Then don't blame me for being polite to her.' His voice was as calm as his expression. 'Nor do I need reminding of my position here, Miss Beauville. The only reason I wanted an introduction to Lord Craxton was because I hadn't seen him around before.'

'So what?' she said rudely. 'It isn't your business to vet everyone who comes to see me.'

'I think it is.'

'I'll remember to give you a detailed guest list for your persual!'

Leaving him treading water, she swam to the far end, and was surprised when she turned round to find him out of the pool, talking to Lila and Johnny. Peeved—it was getting to become a habit, she acknowledged—she did another length and then joined them.

'I thought you were coming in for a swim,' she chided Johnny.

'I didn't realised I'd signed a contract! But if you're anxious to be alone with me, let's take a walk.'

His arm through hers, he led her to the rail that edged the top of the cliff. Far below, the sea foamed gently upon the rocks, and gulls dived and wheeled above the sparkling blue water. A motorboat was moored to the jetty, and it bobbed wildly in the swell of a sudden breeze.

'It looks as if the forecast was right,' Johnny commented. 'They said the weather might break.'

'Why don't we go to St-Paul-de-Vence, then?' Charlotte suggested. 'There's an artist I want to see there.'

'Still searching for a second Picasso?'

'Yes—but it isn't easy. There's no shortage of artists, just a dearth of talent!' She leaned back on the rail. Rayner was looking in their direction and she beckoned him over. 'Lord Craxton's taking me to St-Paul-de-Vence, so you can take the rest of the day off.'

'I realise you'd prefer to go alone,' Rayner said apologetically, 'but I'm afraid I have to drive you.'

'I'm perfectly safe with Lord Craxton.'

'It's my job to accompany you.'

'Let Rayner drive us,' Johnny murmured. 'It's hellishly difficult parking in St-Paul.'

'I want to be alone with you,' she said obstinately, delighted when she saw Rayner's mouth thin.

'Either I drive or you stay here,' he said, ignoring the gibe.

'And if I refuse?' It was a trial of strength, and she was determined to win.

'I'll go to your father.'

'Don't bother. I'll go to him myself and settle this once and for all.'

She ran towards the villa and Johnny caught up with her as she reached the main hall.

'Why make a fuss, Sharly? It doesn't matter if Rayner comes with us.'

'It matters to me. I'm sick of having him watch me night and day.'

'He's only obeying your father's orders.'

But Charlotte was too incensed to listen to reason, and marching into the library, faced her father across the desk.

'That damn man's gone too far,' she fumed. 'I want to fire him!'

Charles Beauville peered at her over his glasses.

'I assume you're referring to Mark?'

'Who else? He's insolent, obstinate and opinionated.'

'Reminds me of a girl I know! And as I've managed to put up with you for twenty-three years, I don't see why you can't do the same with Mark for a few months.'

'A few months? You mean he's only here temporarily?'

'Yes. He—er—he'll be staying until the unrest dies down in Teleguay.'

Instead of being delighted by this piece of news, Charlotte was disconcerted to feel exactly the reverse. Yet a moment ago she had demanded he be fired. Confused by her changeability, she was scared to analyse it.

'I'm sorry you've taken a dislike to him,' her father went on, 'but when he goes I promise you a more conventional chauffeur.'

'Thank you,' she said quietly, and, still disturbed by her feelings, went out.

CHAPTER EIGHT

THE DRIVE to St-Paul-de-Vence took about an hour, for it was Saturday, and traffic was heavier than usual.

Though the glass partition was closed between Mark Rayner and themselves, Charlotte was uncomfortably aware of him. In dark trousers and white shirt, only his peaked cap served to remind her of his status, a fact she found disquieting. She had told him he need not wear his uniform, and this symbol of his role vexed her, for she was convinced he had put it on to rile her, to show he was his own master. What a joke! As if anything she said or did could rob him of his innate self-confidence.

With an effort she concentrated on what Johnny was saying. He had been speaking for several minutes, yet she hadn't heard a word.

'Sorry,' she apologised. 'I was thinking how pleased I am that we came here. I've had enough of sitting round the pool.'

'You mean enough of sitting round the pool watching Lila's seduction act!'

'She's so obvious about it,' Charlotte muttered.

'Is that why you didn't ask her to join us?'

'She wasn't free, anyway. She's having her hair

done. She's going to a gala in Monte Carlo.'

'If you'd like to go, I'm sure I can wangle a couple of tickets.'

'No, thanks. I loathe those sort of functions—everyone dressed to kill and showing off. It's nauseating.'

Johnny's mouth curved up at the corners. 'Not as nauseating as those.' He nodded at the huge billboards enjoining passers-by to smoke particular cigarettes, drive certain cars, enjoy specific soft drinks. 'What a blot on the landscape!'

Charlotte agreed, vaguely recalling when driving along this road had been akin to stepping back into a different century—the muted grey-green of olive trees and darker green of cypresses intermingling on the hills, broken here and there by a red-tiled roof and patches of purple bougainvillaea. Now, modern pink and white stucco villas and apartment blocks sprouted like mushrooms on the slopes, and camping sites bordered the highway, replacing orange and lemon groves.

Yet there were compensations, for today the Riviera was enjoyed by thousands, rather than the rich few who had previously regarded it as an exclusive enclave for their private pleasure.

'We're almost there,' Johnny announced as the grey stone walls and turrets of the ancient town of St-Paul-de-Vence came into view.

It looked as it must have done when it had defended itself from the Moors, who had come across the sea from North Africa. Only as they drew closer did the ravages of time and modern man become apparent. Car fumes polluted the air, transistors destroyed the peace, and thousands of tourists crowded the hilly, narrow cobbled streets, staring through the windows of endless galleries selling derivatives of the Masters, produced in the cellars below or the attics above, at extortionate prices.

Rayner brought the Ferrari to a stop, then slid back the glass partition. 'I can't take the car any higher than this, Miss Beauville. If you'd wait here while I park . . .'

Charlotte nodded and stepped out, standing beside Johnny while Rayner inched his way into a space left by an Audi. It required all his expertise and he did it brilliantly, raising a cheer from a group of youngsters nearby.

Johnny cupped her elbow as they made their way up the steep, cobbled road to the town, Rayner keeping close on the other side of her. She was conscious of other girls eyeing her, no doubt jealous of her two handsome escorts. If only they knew she regarded one as a friend, and the other as . . . Hell, she didn't know what she thought of Rayner.

'Where's this artist you want to see?' Johnny queried.

She rummaged in her bag for a card. 'Nine, rue Breton.'

'I know where that is,' Rayner said, and, noting her surprise, added, 'I stayed here once.'

'Business or pleasure?'

'Pleasurable business.'

With a woman? she wondered, peeved with herself for caring one way or the other.

'You'd better take the lead, then,' she said aloud.

He nodded, but did not leave her side, though he set a faster pace as they mounted the steep incline, turned into an alleyway and began an equally treacherous descent. Charlotte was glad she was wearing flat shoes, but still found it difficult to keep her balance on the cobbles.

'How much further is it, Rayner?'

'We're here.' He indicated an old pine door.

Entering, they found themselves in a typical artisan's *atelier*: a medium-sized room with floor and walls of stone, and light coming in from a large window overlooking the silver-green hillside below. A stocky, black-haired man by an easel came towards them.

'Monsieur Lebrun? I've come to see your work,' Charlotte said in fluent French. 'I was told about you by a friend.'

'A satisfied client, I hope?'

'Why else would I be here?' She smiled.

Pleased by her reply, he began sorting through the canvases stacked around the wall. They were mostly of Provence, painted in luminous colours which captured the spirit of the place.

Charlotte found them extremely good, though Johnny's expression showed the exact opposite. Not so Rayner. He scanned each canvas avidly, a light in his eyes she had never seen before.

'I'll take the lot,' she proclaimed. 'Deliver

them to my villa and I'll pay you for them.'

Monsieur Lebrun was dazed. 'I can't dispose of my entire stock. I'll have nothing left to show other clients?'

'That's the idea,' Charlotte stated. 'I want to buy everything you produce. My lawyers will work out a contract which I'm sure you'll find satisfactory. I'm Charlotte Beauville,' she informed him, and saw his eyes widen at mention of her name. 'Do we have a deal?'

'I'll deliver them tomorrow,' he croaked. 'This is unbelievable. I never dreamed . . . Thank you so much.'

'You're certainly a creature of impulse,' Johnny commented as they wended their way towards the main thoroughfare. 'You'll be telling me next you intend opening your own gallery.'

'I do. It was Rayner's idea, actually, and a very good one.'

'I think it was already in your mind, Miss Beauville,' he interpolated. 'And I'm sure you'll be successful. You have a good eye.'

'I don't think Lord Craxton agrees with you there!'

'I'm a philistine,' Johnny confessed. 'So ignore my opinion!'

They were still laughing at this when they reached the car, and stopped in dismay, for it was boxed in by a Volvo.

'Let's have a drink at the Colombe d'Or and leave Rayner to sort this out,' Johnny said.

Charlotte faced Mark—no, she mustn't think of

him this way. 'Am I allowed to go to the hotel without you?'

He nodded, and as she walked across the road with Johnny she was disconcerted to find Rayner accompanying them. They entered a door set into a high stone wall and found themselves in a large courtyard, with tables and chairs set under gnarled old trees.

'Do you want to sit here or on the terrace?' Johnny asked.

'Here,' Rayner answered for her. 'It's more crowded.'

'Which is why I'd prefer the terrace,' Charlotte said.

'If you sit there, Miss Beauville, I'll have to stay with you, and then we won't get the car freed.'

Recognising the obstinate set of his jaw, she gave in.

'He certainly takes his job seriously,' Johnny commented when they were alone.

'It's what he's paid for,' she sniffed, and stifled a pang of guilt for belittling a man who was conscientious.

'He's an unusual type of man for this kind of job,' Johnny went on when he had ordered their drinks. 'What do you know about him?'

'Only that he came highly recommended. My father wouldn't have engaged him otherwise. Why?'

'Because he reminds me of someone, though it wasn't till a moment ago that I remembered who. General Sir Henry Rayner. I was at school with

Peter, his son, but I know he had an older brother.'

'I can't see it being Rayner,' Charlotte smiled, amused by the very notion.

'Maybe he was born the wrong side of the blanket! Has he ever spoken of his family?'

'Yes. His father *was* in the army, as it happens, and his brother has a smallholding. Oh, and I've just remembered, his mother did sewing of some kind.'

'That settles it, then,' Johnny chuckled. 'Peter—my friend—runs the family estate, and his sister married the Duke of Wallsey and lives in a castle in Scotland.'

'Hardly the type to be Rayner's relatives!' Charlotte sipped her drink. 'What does the older brother do?'

'He's something in the Foreign Office. A bit of a non-conformist, I believe. He dropped from sight for a couple of years and no one quite knew where he went. I heard tell he was in Cuba—which couldn't have pleased his father.' Johnny inclined his head at her empty glass. 'Care for another?'

'No, thanks. Let's see if the car's still boxed in.'

'Where do you fancy having dinner tonight?' Johnny asked as they left the hotel.

'At home. Dad always enjoys seeing you.'

Charlotte's reluctance to go out this evening stemmed from the disquiet she had felt since hearing about General Rayner. She knew Mark couldn't be his son, yet it had served to rekindle her doubts about him, and she preferred to stay in the comfort of familiar surroundings.

Was it possible Mark had faked his references and duped her father? Although they employed a team of people whose sole function was to vet new employees, no one was infallible, and he might have slipped through the net. He might even have been sent here to kidnap her. A chill ran down her spine, and she was glad of Johnny's arm around her shoulders. It gave her a feeling of protection, of safety and normality in a world which suddenly appeared to be slipping off its axis.

Yet, as she saw Mark Rayner coming towards her, her doubts dissolved. If he had wanted to abduct her, he'd not lacked opportunity. They had often been alone outside the villa, including the day he had taken her across the border into Italy to do some shopping, which had provided him with the perfect chance.

'I was coming to fetch you,' he said. 'The car's clear and we can move.'

'Drop me off at my villa, will you, Rayner?' Johnny asked pleasantly as he settled beside Charlotte. 'Make for the Lower Corniche and I'll direct you from there.'

'I know where your home is, m'lord.'

'Don't tell me you've been—what's the expression—casing the joint?'

'I'm afraid I have. It's my business to know the layout of all the houses Miss Beauville might visit.'

Staggered by this information, Johnny closed the partition and stared at Charlotte. 'Anything going on I don't know about?'

'The revolution in Teleguay.'

'Ah, now it makes sense. But wouldn't it be safer for you to stay home till it's been put down?'

'And if the rebels win, what then? Do I remain a prisoner in the villa?'

He frowned, clearly disturbed, and was still mulling it over when the car purred to a stop outside the door of a grand three-storey villa set in several hectares of wooded land high above Nice.

'Coming in to say hello to my mother?' he asked.

'Not today,' Charlotte begged off. 'I want to change, too—and I take longer than you to make myself presentable!'

'You're always perfect to me,' he said, kissing her on the cheek. 'See you around eight-thirty.'

'Shall Rayner collect you?' she offered. 'You've left your car at our place.'

'No sweat. I'll take a cab.'

She signalled Rayner to drive off, and as the house disappeared from sight she ordered him to stop and joined him in the front.

'Did you think I was hasty this afternoon, buying Lebrun's entire output?' she asked when they were on their way again.

'Having second thoughts?'

'Not about the quality of the paintings. But the magnitude of the undertaking is rather daunting.'

'I can't see why. You're conversant with the art world, and you can afford to employ the best people to advise you. Anyway, Lebrun's work is highly saleable.'

'You sound quite knowledgeable yourself.'

'Art isn't the prerogative of the rich.' Mark Rayner's tone was dry. 'I may not have the money to buy what I like, but there's no charge for appreciation.'

She deserved the put-down, and acknowledged it. 'I'm sorry. I didn't mean to sound condescending.'

He flashed her a look from eyes which humour had turned silver-grey. 'Things are improving. Three weeks ago you wouldn't even have admitted it!'

If he had bestowed the warmest possible compliment on her, she couldn't have been more delighted. Was it because she was aware of his disapproval that his approbation meant so much to her? She gave him a sidelong glance and saw his mouth quirk before he looked quickly away.

'What will you do this evening?' she asked. 'I'm dining at home, so you'll be free.'

'I'll probably see a friend.'

'I didn't realise you knew anyone down here.'

'You know very little about me, Miss Beauville.'

It was another put-down, and though she burned with shame she hid it behind an indifferent shrug. But her lack of interest was a pretence, and she wondered if he was intimating that he had a chequered past. One thing she was certain of: he always had his guard up, monitoring everything he said and did. Her doubts about him multiplied, and she was relieved when the gates of the villa loomed in sight.

During dinner she discussed her new venture with her father, and was pleased when he gave it his unqualified approval.

'If you take my advice, you'll open a gallery locally,' he said. 'You can always widen your horizons when you've gained some experience. Besides, if you get egg on your face, only the locals will be able to make a meal of it!'

Charlotte burst out laughing. 'What do you think, Johnny?'

'I think your father has a point. Why not see if there's anything going in Cannes? What with the Film Festival and the hordes that come in its wake, it's an ideal venue.'

She nodded thoughtfully. 'They're certainly the right type of customer—money no object and an anxiety to show how cultured they are!'

For the rest of the evening they discussed the venture, and it was past midnight when Johnny said goodnight and she walked with him to his car.

'Any chance of seeing you tomorrow?' he quizzed.

'I'm afraid not.'

'I'll call you, anyway.'

Drawing her into his arms, he kissed her hard on the mouth. She wished she could respond to him, but refused to pretend, reluctant to show him any encouragement. After a moment he released her and gave a lop-sided grin.

'I'm a glutton for punishment, aren't I?'

'I'm sorry, Johnny.'

'Me, too. But I won't give up trying—not until you tell me you're in love with another man.'

'That wasn't exactly a lingering farewell,' her father commented when she rejoined him. 'Don't tell me he's gone the way of Barry?'

'Don't tell me you fancy a titled son-in-law?' she joshed.

'Frankly, I'd approve of anyone who makes you happy.'

'*Anyone*?' She widened her eyes at him. 'Then perhaps I'll marry Rayner!'

Charles Beauville abruptly set down his brandy glass. 'He hasn't taken advantage of his position to——'

'No, no,' she said hastily. 'I was joking.'

But was she? Musing on it later, as she lay in bed, she wasn't sure. Mark Rayner was handsome, intelligent and entertaining. Equally important, he wasn't intimidated by her, which was more than could be said for most of the men she knew. He also excited her physically. Memories of the way he had touched and kissed her the night she had left Barry in the restaurant set her pulses racing, and she felt an urge for him touch her again.

Mortified, she buried her head in her pillow. Such thoughts were crazy. He meant nothing to her, and to him she was merely a wage packet. If he said anything different she wouldn't believe him—would she?

It was a question she asked herself over and over again, and she was no nearer an answer when she fell asleep.

CHAPTER NINE

CHARLOTTE awoke with a start. Moonlight streamed into the room, casting a swathe of silver across the foot of her bed, and she yawned and stretched, unexpectedly restless.

Switching on the bedside-lamp, she reached for a book, but after reading a page she flung it aside, unable to concentrate. The night was silent except for the faint sound of the sea lapping against the shoreline, and the soughing of the breeze in the palms, and she had an urge to run barefoot through the grass.

She recollected Rayner calling her capricious, and wondered what he would make of her thoughts. Probably dismiss them as childish. Yet perhaps she was being unfair. He had taken her announcement to open a gallery seriously enough. What a pity he wouldn't be here to see it come to fruition.

A slight breeze cleared a puff of cloud shading the moon, and the sudden brightness gave sparkle to the stars in their black velvet bed. The jewelled clock beside her showed half-past two and, reaching for the filmy silk dressing-gown that matched her nightdress, she went down to the garden.

103

Reaching the rail that bordered the cliff, she stared out at the sea. Moonlight silvered the edges of the waves, and far out on the horizon gleamed the faint lights of a yacht—Johnny's or Barry's, perhaps, though Barry himself might be on his way back to the States. He had called her several times after she had walked out on him, but she had refused to see him.

A dog barked in the distance and she jumped nervously, but this was nothing to the fear that shivered through her as a dark figure moved away from the darker shadow of a tree and stealthily glided towards her.

'D-don't come any further,' she quavered, 'or I'll shoot.'

'And kill your chauffeur? Surely not, Miss Beauville?'

Mark Rayner stepped into the moonlight, and she glared at him. 'How dare you creep up on me like that?'

'You deserved it. Don't you know better than to be out here alone?'

'Hardly alone,' she snapped. 'The grounds are well-guarded.'

'Then how come you were petrified when you heard me?'

There was no answer to this, and she didn't attempt one. Instead she went on the attack. 'If you're so concerned for my safety, you should have been here yourself.'

'I didn't anticipate your requiring me at two in the morning,' he said softly.

'But you're here, aren't you? Why *are* you

wandering about so late?'

'I was checking the security before turning in.'

'You mean you've just got back? You're very late.'

'I wasn't aware I had to be in by a specific hour.'

She ignored his comment. 'Did you meet your friend?'

'No. I had dinner alone in the harbour in Nice.'

'What a pity Lila wasn't free!'

'I've already told you, she doesn't interest me.'

The flatness of his voice warned Charlotte she was treading on dangerous ground but, like a dog gnawing a bone, she went on regardless.

'Was it one of the girls you met at my party?'

'I never said it was a girl.'

' "I never said it was a girl",' she mimicked. 'Can't you give a straight answer to a straight question?'

'When it's your concern I can.'

'Meaning it's none of my business?'

A slight smile curved his mouth. 'You have to admit you sound more than a little jealous!'

Her heart skipped a beat, then pounded furiously. 'I thought I'd made it plain I never mess with the hired help!'

Tossing her head, she ran swiftly past him, so swiftly that she stumbled and would have fallen had he not reached out for her.

'Thanks,' she said carelessly, and went to pull away. But his grip tightened and he drew her closely against him, the hardness of his body pressing upon hers, the steely strength of his thighs rigid against her own.

'What's the hurry, Miss Beauville? Scared of getting contaminated?'

Nervously she met his eyes. The moonlight kindled them into glowing charcoal flames, giving him a sinister quality that sent the blood rushing turbulently through her veins.

'Leave go of me!' she ordered, trying to wriggle free.

'That isn't what your heart's saying.' His arms still bound her, his mouth so close to hers that his breath was warm on her lips. 'How fast it's beating . . . like the wings of a bird trying to escape its bars. Do you feel trapped, sweet Charlotte—or should I call you sweet vixen?—for they snap and snarl from bravado, too?'

'I don't care what you call me,' she rasped, forcing herself to remain supine in the hope that if she relaxed he might come to his senses. 'But don't do anything you'll regret.'

'Don't you mean anything *you'll* regret?'

Before she had a chance to answer, his mouth fastened on hers. As before, there was no gradual build-up of emotion, only a raw passion which seared through her like fire.

'I'll show you how it feels to be loved by a man,' he said thickly, 'not those schoolboys you're used to.' His mouth left hers and travelled over her cheek to her ear. She shivered as his tongue gently licked her lobe, then tantalisingly probed deeper. 'Sweet Charlotte,' he whispered urgently. 'Darling, adorable Charlotte!'

He kissed her again, but this time with slow deliberation, teasing, taunting, nibbling, until all resistance left her and she clung to him, her lips parting wide, her trembling body signalling acquiescence.

Again and again his tongue plundered the warm moistness within, while his hands moved sensuously across her back and over her spine, caressing her shoulders, her waist, the rounding curve of her hips.

Time ceased as he unhurriedly explored her, encouraging her by his very control to lose the last remaining vestige of hers. She made no attempt to stop him when he undid the ribbons of her dressing-gown, and as his hands sought and found her breasts they swelled to his touch. Every part of her longed to be held, to feel his skin upon hers, his thighs pressing close, his hardness inside her.

'I want you,' he muttered thickly. 'Put your hands on me, darling. Hold me.'

The rawness of his passion excited and scared her, warning her that if she gave in to her desires she would be taking a fatal step. And she didn't dare; she wasn't ready for it.

She tried to pull away from him but he refused to release her, and frenziedly she clawed at his face. But instead of skin she felt the thick silkiness of his hair, and longed to run her fingers through it, to feel its downy softness on her breasts.

She tried to gather strength against her weakening resolve and, sensing it, he swung her into his arms and strode towards the steps.

'W-where are you t-taking me?' she stammered.

'To the poolhouse.'

'No! No!'

'Shall we go to your room?' he demanded bluntly.

For answer she kicked out wildly, hoping to make him drop her. 'Put me down!'

'What will you do if I refuse—fire me!' He gave a throaty chuckle. 'Frankly, I don't care if you do. Making love to you will be worth it.'

'You're mad! Put me down and I'll forget the whole thing. Rayner, please, I promise I won't fire you.'

Ignoring her cry, he tightened his hold and increased his stride. Terror gripped her, stifling thought, but as they reached the pool and she saw the white gleam of the poolhouse she gave a soft murmur and came to life. Clasping him round the neck, she tilted her face to his.

'Kiss me,' she whispered. 'Kiss me.'

Surprised, he half lowered his head, and instantly she pulled his face down to hers and bit him hard on the lip.

Shock, as much as pain, stopped him in his tracks. 'You bitch!' he ground out, blood trickling down his chin.

'You asked for it.'

'And you've asked for *this*.' Stepping to the edge of the pool, he raised her in his arms, held her there motionless, then dropped her into the water.

Charlotte sank like a stone, then came up gasping for air.

'You . . . you . . .' Coughing and spluttering, she swam to the side, no easy task with her sodden nightclothes hampering her every movement. But Rayner stood silently by, making no attempt to offer a helping hand until she started to climb the steps.

'Countess Dracula, I presume!' There was a hint of laughter in his voice. 'I must remember not to kiss you when there's a full moon!'

Derisively she brushed his arm aside. 'You're despicable!'

'I'm sorry you feel that.'

'How do you expect me to feel? Grateful?' Water dripped from her hair and her clothes, forming a puddle around her bare feet—her gold kid slippers were floating forlornly in the middle of the pool. Aware what an unattractive, sorry figure she made only served to fuel her rage. 'I'll pay you back for this if it's the last thing I do!'

'You brought it on yourself,' he declared. 'There was no need to take a chunk out of me.' Gingerly he put a hand to his mouth, wincing as he touched it. It was easy to see why. His lower lip was swollen and bleeding. 'A nip would have been equally as effective.'

Charlotte's fury rose higher. He was a fine one to talk. Hadn't his response been equally savage? If he'd been a gentleman, he'd simply have set her down on her feet.

'A nip wouldn't have stopped you,' she grated. 'You're too convinced you're irresistible.'

He inclined his head. 'You're beginning to make

me think I'm not!'

'I'm glad you've finally acknowledged it.'

'After tonight, I'd be a fool not to.' His eyes moved from her breasts—visible through the clinging wet silk of her nightgown—to her face. 'Don't they say once bitten, twice shy?'

Shards of silver flecked the deep-set grey eyes, but she doubted whether they held humour, despite the quip.

'I hope you won't let this affect our relationship,' he went on. 'I have no option but to stay for the next few weeks, so I suggest we try to be civil to each other.'

'Civil?' It was difficult for her to even say the word. 'I don't ever intend speaking to you again, other than to fire you!'

'Your father won't allow it,' he said implacably.

'It won't stop me trying.'

'What excuse will you give?'

The implication that it wouldn't be the truth made Charlotte wary. She hadn't exactly been a passive partner in tonight's episode, and it was foolish to pretend otherwise.

'I'll think of something,' she countered.

One well-shaped eyebrow rose. 'You mean you'll lie?'

'Wait and see.'

Without another word she slipped past him and ran up the steps. They were gritty on her bare feet, but she was beyond caring. Mark Rayner had made her look a stupid fool, and that hurt far more than the rough stone on her soles.

Alone in her room, she stripped and went under the shower, its needle-point force easing her tension. Relaxed, she snuggled beneath the silk sheets and closed her eyes.

Sleep refused to come, and her thoughts strayed to Rayner and the necessity to get him out of her life. Yes, out of her life. No point mincing words. Tonight she had gone a step nearer the brink than when he had previously kissed her, and who was to say that on the next occasion—she didn't doubt there would be one, despite her brave words—her resistance might crumble completely? Because she was still a virgin it did not make her a saint.

But she had always believed passion and marriage should be intertwined and, until Mark Rayner's advent in her life, had never questioned her beliefs. Now she was doing more: taking a long, hard look at the girl she was, and the girl she was likely to become if she went on in the self same way.

She thumped her pillow into a more comfortable position. Looking at herself with a jaundiced eye, she saw she was headstrong and domineering, and that only a man of sufficiently strong character could be her equal. In that respect her vast wealth had weakened her relationships with most of the men she knew, for they were in awe of her position, which was enough to kill her feelings for them stone dead. But in Mark Rayner she had met her match. He might be prepared to marry her for her money, but she could never use it to rule him!

Horrified at where her thoughts were taking her,

she knew that as long as he remained here he was a constant threat to her peace of mind. Yet how to be rid of him? What reason could she give her father to dismiss him? His confidence in Mark's ability was absolute, and as long as he believed this nonsense about the revolutionaries in Teleguay being a threat to her he would insist on Mark remaining at her side day and night.

No, however hard she searched for a solution, it was impossible to have him fired by fair means—which meant she had to achieve it by foul!

CHAPTER TEN

MARK did not remember when he had felt more furious with himself. Of all the irresponsible things to do, his behaviour tonight had been the worst. Until now, no woman had succeeded in making him lose his self-control if he hadn't wanted to, yet tonight a spoilt young girl had done exactly that!

Charlotte had set out to vamp him, of course. He had realised it as soon as she had questioned him about where he had been that evening. Yet it had been no excuse for his subsequent behaviour.

Bathing his sore lip, he ruefully acknowledged that she had come out the victor. And thank heaven she had! If not . . . He groaned as he considered the consequences. Regardless of the fact that she had deliberately provoked and aroused him, he would have had to resign from the service.

Thankful to be spared such a decision, he dried his lip gingerly and padded over to the window. All was dark and quiet, which was more than could be said for his mood! The passion that had fired him earlier had abated, not died, and it was necessary to curb his thoughts. What in hell was wrong with him that a spoilt bitch should make him feel like an adolescent schoolboy?

113

The knowledge that she was lying in bed in her room on the floor below stirred his loins, and he swore quietly but fluently. Watch it, he warned himself. You have a job to do, a very special job, so don't blow it because of voluptuous breasts and silken thighs that you want to bury your head in . . .

A shiver brought him from his reverie, and he realised he was still standing at the window with his wet towel draped around his waist.

'That damn girl will give me pneumonia on top of everything else!' he muttered, and, throwing his towel on a chair, slid between the sheets.

Charlotte, in the room below, woke early and carefully plotted her revenge on Mark Rayner.

She dressed with great calculation, satisfied that her simple white dress, with its scooped neckline and full skirt, made her look young and innocent. Heck, she *was* young and innocent, though not for long, if that damned 'minder' had his way with her!

She was trying not to think of this when she went on to the terrace, her red-gold hair flowing around her shoulders like a curtain of flame, her eyes, privy to her secret thoughts, gleaming like emeralds.

The object of her machinations stood in the shade of a marble pillar, black trousers drawing attention to muscular thighs, white shirt a foil for bronzed skin.

'Good morning, Rayner,' she said casually, waving a hand in his direction as she poured herself a fruit juice. She sensed he was taken aback by her calmness, and guessed he had expected her to throw a tantrum at the sight of him. Pleased she had jolted him, she threw him a friendly smile, as if the interlude in the garden had never taken place. 'Had breakfast?'

'No, Miss Beauville.'

'Then join me.'

It was not the first occasion she had invited him to do so, and he took a chair opposite her.

'What are your plans today?' he asked.

'I'm staying by the pool, and a few friends are dropping by later.' She poured cream into her coffee and idly stirred it. 'Your lip looks swollen.' She stared at her cup as if embarrassed. 'I'm sorry I hurt you.'

'I deserved it, miss. I can only blame the moonlight and your beauty. Both bewitched me.'

She raised her head, her green eyes limpid. 'What an enchanting thing to say, Rayner.'

'It isn't to butter you up, Miss Beauville. I mean it.'

'Thank you. And in case you're worried I'll have you fired, I'd like you to know I've changed my mind. I have confidence in your ability to take care of me, and I'm sure you won't repeat last night's behaviour.'

'Never. I give you my word on that.'

His relief was palpable, and Charlotte hid her delight. It was important to set his mind at rest; only then could her plan work.

'A property agent rang me this morning,' she

went on idly. 'He heard from Monsieur Lebrun that I'm looking for a gallery, and has arranged to show me one in Cannes tomorrow morning.'

'I hope you settle on one before I leave,' Rayner said. 'I'd enjoy seeing your success.'

'It might be a ghastly flop,' she warned. 'The previous owners went bust.'

'I can't see your father letting that happen to you.'

'Shows how little you know him! If I can't run the gallery at a profit, he'd stand by and let me close it.'

'I bet you'd be furious!'

'On the contrary. I'd be furious if I thought he was indulging me. It's because I know how tough he can be that I'll get a kick out of showing him I can accomplish something on my own.' She pushed back her chair. 'I'll see you at the pool.'

When she joined him, Rayner was in the middle of his twenty lengths, but when he emerged he appeared no more out of breath than if he had completed only one. No man had the right to be so attractive, she mused as he raked his hair smooth with a strong but well-shaped hand. He drew up a chair a few yards from hers and relaxed on it. But there was an alert air about him, like a panther ready to strike at the first sense of danger.

'I'm bored,' she pronounced. 'Let's play our game.'

This consisted of choosing a controversial subject, usually from one of the morning papers, and tossing a coin to see which side each of them should defend. But today neither of them had read the papers, and she switched on the radio to hear if there was an item of news they might debate. The name 'Teleguay' caught their attention. The rebels had finally won control, and General Vargar had declared himself Head of State.

'Have you ever been to South America, Rayner?' Charlotte asked.

'Not unless you count Acapulco,' he smiled, 'which is like any other luxury resort in the sun.'

'Did you go with one of your employers?'

'Yes.'

'You must be well-travelled. I suppose your family followed your father abroad when you were young?'

'Sometimes.'

'I wonder if he came across a General Rayner,' she said casually, watching his face. 'He might even be a relation!'

'A general?' Rayner chuckled and shook his head. 'Do you know him, then?'

'No. But Johnny—Lord Craxton—mentioned him yesterday. He was at school with one of the General's sons. Quite a coincidence you having the same surname,' she added slyly.

'It's not an uncommon one. There are upper-class Rayners as well as plebeian ones.'

Charlotte didn't know how to pursue the subject without making her curiosity obvious, so she changed tack completely and suggested they went water-skiing.

'I'd rather we stayed on terra firma for the next

few days,' he said.

'Afraid I'll be snatched at sea?'

'It's a possibility.'

She giggled at the notion. 'There's such a thing as being too conscientious.'

'Not with the salary *I'm* getting.'

His answer was a nasty jolt, reminding her that his solicitude was bought, his concern for her merely the result of a hefty pay-cheque. Yet she had always known this, so why should she be hurt?

Leaving his side, she climbed to the top of the diving-board and somersaulted into the water. For the next hour she did dive after dive, each one performed with exact precision. Rayner made no attempt to join her, watching from the edge, arms folded across his chest.

Was he as aware of her body as she was of his? she wondered as she climbed the board for the nth time. She found she was trembling, and hurriedly raised her arms above her head to dive.

'I think you've done enough for one day,' he called. 'Come and rest.'

Astonished at his ordering her what to do, she was on the verge of telling him what *he* could do when she remembered her plan. Putting him in his place might be sweet, but the revenge she had in store tomorrow was going to be even sweeter.

'I *was* feeling tired,' she admitted prettily as she reached his side. 'But once I start practising I forget to stop. You're a solicitous "minder", Rayner. I'll ask my father to give you a raise.'

A flush darkened his skin. 'I don't need extra

money for warning you when you're overdoing things, Miss Beauville.'

Gratified that she had cut him down to size, she settled on her sun-bed and closed her eyes.

Later in the afternoon a dozen or so of her friends arrived, including Johnny and Lila and, as dusk fell and the sun sank in a blaze of orange into the purple velvet horizon, a champagne buffet was served by the pool.

Rayner kept discreetly in the background, as usual—to the chagrin of Lila and Charlotte's other girlfriends. But Charlotte herself was conscious of him watching her, an unusual warmth in his eyes. Lust, she thought dismissively. Her rejection of him last night had challenged his ego, a challenge no man as confident as this one could ignore.

Boldly she met his eyes, encouraging him to believe she accepted his presence without rancour. Deception did not come easily to her, but her determination to be rid of him once and for all made her pose easier.

'When my friends come over again you must join us and not stand on the sidelines,' she told him as the last Porsche disappeared down the driveway at three a.m. 'It's silly for me to go on treating you as an ordinary chauffeur when you're clearly nothing of the sort.'

'I appreciate the suggestion, Miss Beauville, but it's easier for me to do my job if I'm not distracted socially.'

'As you please.' One foot on the steps, she paused. 'Oh—I nearly forgot to tell you. The estate agent phoned while I was changing, and I'm meeting him at the gallery at ten tomorrow, so have the car ready at nine-thirty.'

'Do you think——' Rayner stopped, then shook his head as if he'd thought better of it.

'Yes?' she queried, eyes wide. 'You were saying?'

'Nothing. Just a passing thought.' Yet his face had a strained, preoccupied air she hadn't seen before.

Wait until tomorrow, she gloated as she mounted the stairs. Whatever worries Mark Rayner had now would be doubled when he awoke to find she had taken off for Cannes on her own!

CHAPTER ELEVEN

FOOT hard on the accelerator, Charlotte hurtled along the road, intent on putting as much distance as possible between herself and the villa before Mark Rayner realised she had gone. There was no telling how soon that would be; she peered anxiously in the driving mirror, relieved to see no sign of the Ferrari behind her.

When her father learned how easily she had given Rayner the slip, he would send him packing. Which was precisely what she wanted! That would teach him not to make unwanted advances to any female employer in the future.

She slowed down as she reached a bend, then shot forward again. There was an acrid smell of burning rubber as the brake linings protested at such harsh treatment, but she ignored it. A cyclist careered out from a turning on her right, and she hit the brakes so hard that the Lotus almost stood up.

The bike swerved into a hedge to avoid the side of the car, and the man fell off. Charlotte was tempted to stop and apologise, but was scared Rayner was on her tail, and shouted, '*Excusez-moi, monsieur*,' then roared on.

Ignoring the coast road, she took the shorter

route to Cannes. She still had to go through Juan-les-Pins, and was reminded of the night she had come here with Mark Rayner. She had only known him a few short weeks, yet he seemed to have changed her entire perspective on life, maturing her to a degree she had never anticipated.

Blanking out the thought, she concentrated on the road. The boat-filled harbour of Golfe-Juan came and went, and soon tall apartment blocks heralded the approach to Cannes.

Bypassing the one-way shopping centre of the rue d'Antibes, she headed for the Croisette, which was bordered on one side by glittering hotels and on the other by a wide stretch of promenade and beach. How well-tended everything was. Even the fronds of the palms were shining, and the beaches had been swept clean. Only the mass of parked cars was evidence of too many people on too small a stretch of land.

Miraculously a parking space appeared, and she backed into it before it was snatched from her. Only then did she draw a satisfied breath. It was barely nine o'clock, and considering Rayner hadn't got to bed till three-thirty—he always reconnoitred the grounds before turning in—he would just be stirring.

Had she but known it, the object of her thoughts was already showered and dressed and clipping his gun into the holster beneath his arm. It felt hard and cold against his skin, but by the time he reached the downstairs hall he was unaware of it. Charlotte was nowhere to be seen, and he strode smartly to the four-car garage.

She had not put in an appearance when he drew the Ferrari to a stop at the front door, and his mouth curved wryly. He had thought she was over-optimistic promising to be ready at nine-thirty. Ten-thirty, more likely! Resignedly he climbed out and leaned against the bonnet, waiting.

Twenty minutes went by and wry humour turned to ire. Surely she was awake by now, so why hadn't she sent word she was going to be late? Another ten minutes passed, and he was debating whether to go in search of her maid, when the woman came through the hall.

'*Mademoiselle est partie*,' Maria said.

'No, she hasn't,' Mark replied. 'I arranged to meet her here.'

Maria raised her eyes heavenwards, and with a muttered curse Mark jumped into the car and roared down the drive. This was Charlotte's way of paying him back for his behaviour the other night. He had forced his kisses on her and shown her he was her master, and she was now making it clear it had been a very temporary situation.

Fear gripped his stomach. Didn't she understand the danger she was in? His neck would be on the block if anything happened to her. He prayed she'd have the sense to keep her foot hard on the accelerator if she were ambushed. Her Lotus went like a bomb if properly handled.

Rage and fear compounded in him and he bent low over the wheel, disregarding the speed limit as he jumped the lights, narrowly missed a bus and hurtled down the rue d'Antibes towards Cannes. If any police were around, he'd be a goner. He could always give them a number to ring—for security reasons he carried no credentials on him—but before they'd satisfied themselves precious moments would be lost. Damn Charlotte! When he finally got his hands on her, he'd shake her till her teeth rattled!

Charlotte meanwhile was strolling past the Martinez and Carlton hotels towards the Galerie Rosalia, which stood between a furrier and a jewellery store.

'Mademoiselle Beauville?' A swarthy-faced young man greeted her at the plate-glass door. 'Alphonse Gizzer at your service. I think you'll find this gallery exactly what you're looking for.'

She preceded him into a large, empty room with three stairs leading to a mezzanine level at the back. A leisurely tour followed, and she was about to ply him with questions when the door opened behind her.

Mark Rayner stood silhouetted against the outside glare. That he was in a towering rage was evidenced by the square set of his jaw and the ominous glitter in his eyes. Her heart skipped a beat and began pounding furiously. Don't be crazy, she admonished herself. He works for you, not the other way round!

'You managed to find me?' she commented casually.

'It didn't require a clairvoyant.' His voice was deceptively quiet. 'Your car stood out a mile—in more ways than one. Remind me to give you lessons in parking.'

Aware of the agent watching them, she shrugged. 'Now you're here, what do you think of the place?'

'I'll tell you what I think when we're alone,' he said meaningfully.

Ignoring him, she spoke to Monsieur Gizzer. 'The position's perfect, but I don't think it's large enough for my requirements.'

'That can easily be solved,' came the instant reply. 'The lease of the people upstairs expires in a few months, and you can have first option.'

'Is it the same size as this?'

'Yes, but with a different layout, I brought the plans to show you.' He opened his briefcase and rummaged through some papers, then clicked his teeth. 'I appear to have left them in the office. I'll go and collect them.'

'I'll come with you,' Charlotte volunteered.

'It's better if we study them here. Then I can explain everything.' The agent glanced at the chauffeur. 'If you drive me, I'll be back sooner.'

'Get a taxi,' Mark Rayner said. 'If you aren't back in fifteen minutes, we're leaving.'

As the man hurried out, Charlotte glared at Rayner. 'There was no need to be rude to the poor man. I've no intention of leaving until I see the plans.' She stared around. 'This place might do. The lighting is wrong but——'

'I'm more concerned with what's wrong with you!' he cut in. 'What were you trying to prove by giving me the slip?'

'That I'm capable of taking care of myself and don't need *you*.' She waved an arm around her. 'Can you see any kidnappers lurking in the corners?'

'That doesn't mean you weren't followed and aren't being watched,' he stormed. 'Vargar's men might——'

'You're trying to scare me so you can hold on to your job! But when my father hears about this morning, you'll be out on your ear!'

'On the contrary. For the next two months I'll be sticking to you closer than glue to a stamp. Regardless of what you think of me, your father agrees I'm the best man for the job.'

'I *won't* have you breathing down my neck,' she raged. 'I'd rather be dead than live like a prisoner!'

'That might be your only choice,' he said wearily. 'Can't you get it into your head that as of now you're a prime target?'

'General Vargar has more sense than to have me abducted,' she asserted loftily. 'If my father pulled out of Teleguay, the economy would collapse.'

'Not if they forced him to go on running the mines for *their* benefit.'

'He'd never do that!'

'If they had you as a hostage, he'd agree to anything.' Rayner came a step closer. 'For heaven's sake, listen to me.'

'Why?'

'Because I care about your safety. Because I care about *you*.' With a muffled exclamation, he caught her shoulders. 'Don't you realise that?'

Charlotte was at a loss what to say. If he was making a declaration of love, why did he sound angry?

'Lord knows, I've fought against it,' he went on in the same rough voice, 'but I can't help myself. I love you.'

'Don't you mean lust?' she murmured.

'Unfortunately it's love,' he sighed. 'Even though there are times when I could strangle you!''

'How charming!'

'Love doesn't blind me to your faults.' He glowered at her. 'You're the first woman who's got under my skin. You amuse me, intrigue me, provoke me until I don't know whether I'm on my head or my heels. The only thing I'm sure of is that life without you would be untenable.'

Hearing his impassioned declaration, Charlotte felt afraid and lost. Afraid of the forces she had unleashed, and lost because part of her wanted to believe him, and part of her couldn't.

'It's no use,' she said gently. 'There can—there can never be anything between us.'

'Maybe this will change your mind.'

Swift as an eagle, he swooped and covered her mouth with his. His lips were hard and demanding, as were the hands that roved down her back to her waist, moulding her to his body. Heat radiated from him, and she smelled his spicy aftershave and the more personal scent of the man—evoking images of forest and pine trees, of moonlight and stars. She tried to resist him but was powerless to prevent the wave of passion that swept her high and tossed her into a sea of desire. Racked by longing, she wanted him to be part of her, and was uncaring of the morrow and the problems it would bring.

'I'll never get enough of you,' he whispered upon her lips, his fingers caressing her neck and pausing at the top button of her sundress. He made no effort to undo it, and she found this disconcerting. How much easier to despise him for being brutal than to love him for being tender.

Was that why he was holding back? To convince her he truly cared for her, and that the prize of capturing Charles Beauville's daughter meant nothing to him?

Bitterness soured her desire, giving her the will-power to resist him, and though she didn't physically push him away—he was too strong for her to do that—he sensed her emotional withdrawal. Slowly he lifted his mouth from hers, though his body remained close.

'Why are you scared of believing me?' he asked, his lips a breath away from hers. 'I know you aren't indifferent to me.'

'Because I flirted with you? Grow up, Rayner! We've nothing in common. If you'd please let me go . . .'

'Not yet. I've a few more things to say. I love you, and I don't want you thinking that my behaviour the other night means I don't respect you. If I've no respect for anyone, it's myself. I've never lost control before, but then I've never felt for a woman as I feel for you.'

'Now *that* I believe,' she said sarcastically. 'I'm young, desirable and rich beyond your wildest dreams. So why shouldn't you want me?'

'I'd be happier if you didn't have a penny.'

She laughed. 'You really do take me for a fool, don't you?'

'I take you for a girl who doesn't believe she can be loved for herself.'

'Certainly not by you!'

Anger lit silver shards in his eyes. 'Carry on as you are, and no one in their right mind will love you! At the moment you're young enough to make something of yourself. But if you go on mixing with jet-set idiots, you'll——'

'Will marrying you save me?' she mocked. 'Will I learn about real life living in your family mansion, or do you intend moving into mine?'

'Stop it,' he grated, clutching her by her hair and jerking her head back.

'You're hurting me!' she cried.

'That makes two of us. Look into my eyes and tell me you think I'm lying to you.'

She wanted to do exactly that, yet staring into the grey depths she found it impossible. 'I'm sorry if I've led you on, Mark,' she murmured, saying his name aloud for the first time. 'But—but though I'm attracted to you, I don't love you. You're too much of a mystery to me.'

His lids lowered, giving his face a shuttered expression. 'Your father doesn't mistrust me. Isn't that enough for you?'

'He doesn't have a woman's intuition. I think you're playing a double game and you're not what you seem. You may even be planning to kidnap me yourself. If you——'

His hand suddenly covered her mouth, his body tense as a tiger. Her eyes sparked fury, though it turned to fear as she saw his features grow harder, tougher, infinitely more ruthless. As if in slow motion, his other hand carefully moved towards his armpit.

'I wouldn't do that if I were you,' a guttural male voice said. 'Not unless you wish to have your head blown off.'

Charlotte gasped and Mark Rayner flashed her a warning, though he remained motionless as a statue.

'Is this a hold-up?' he asked in a bored tone.

'Yes, my friend. So turn round very slowly.'

As he did, Charlotte saw a stocky man in the centre of the room. He was olive-skinned, his pock-marked faced decorated with a heavy black moustache and equally heavy eyebrows.

'That's better,' the man said. 'Now take out your gun very carefully and drop it on the floor.'

Charlotte waited to see if Mark would make a fight of it, and was astounded when he spoke in a subdued voice. 'I don't want any trouble. We'll give you all the money we have on us, and forget we ever saw you.'

'We don't want money. Now step back from Miss Beauville.'

'How do you know my name?' Charlotte

demanded.

'I know *everything* about you,' the man replied. 'You've been my pet subject for months.'

'What do you want?' she asked.

'You know very well. That's why *he's* here.' The gun waggled in Mark's direction. 'To take care of you. And he did a great job until today.' The man paused as two others, equally dark and saturnine, came into the gallery.

'Ready, Parek?' the one nearest the door called.

Parek nodded and motioned to Charlotte. 'Go over to Lucca and link your arm through his. He has a gun, too, so don't try anything stupid. We don't want to kill you, but we will if we have to. As for you . . .' Parek regarded Mark, his index finger curling on the trigger of his gun.

'Don't kill him!' Charlotte said shrilly. 'If you do, I'll make a dash for it and you'll have to kill me, too.'

'Be quiet,' Mark ordered.

'I won't. If that swine harms you, I'll put up a fight. And no matter what he says, I'm no use to him dead.'

'Come on, Parek,' Lucca called impatiently. 'Gizzer can't wait outside for ever.'

Muttering angrily, Parek lowered his gun, and Charlotte—knowing how easily her victory might have turned to tragedy—went over to the man by the door. He was taller and thinner than Parek, with a fleshy nose and lank hair. He gripped her arm tightly, and the younger man beside him, his eyes hidden by pebble lenses, pressed against the other side of her, close enough for her to smell the sweat of his fear.

Glancing round, she saw Parek fling an arm across Mark's shoulder as though they were the best of friends, and together they all stepped outside. The pavement was thronged with people, cars slowly cruised along the Croisette, and holidaymakers strolled out from their hotels and crossed the road to the beach.

A blue Citroën was parked by the kerb, Alphonse Gizzer—the man from the agency—at the wheel. Charlotte and Mark were pushed into the back, with Lucca and pebble lenses—she heard someone call him Borra—sitting either side of them. Parek took the front passenger seat, and at once the Citroën pulled out into the stream of traffic.

Parek was the oldest of the group and the leader, for he alone gave commands. He and Lucca might be Libyans, though Gizzer and Borrá were lighter-skinned. In the driving mirror she saw Gizzer's eyes. They were almost fawn in colour and dull as mud. Killer's eyes, she thought, and felt a stab of fear.

'You won't get away with this,' Mark said.

'We already have,' Parek grinned. 'Kidnapping Miss Beauville was the hardest part. Keeping her will be easy.'

They gathered speed and Parek spoke to Gizzer. Charlotte's heart gave a violent thump. They were Teleguayan! So Mark was right! She strained to hear what was being said.

'Why did we have to bring the man along?' Gizzer was demanding. 'That means two to watch.'

'Get on with the driving and leave the decisions to me,' Parek retorted.

Charlotte sidled a glance at Mark. Did he understand what the men were saying? He had spent time in Acapulco, so might have sufficient knowledge of Spanish to follow it.

What was going through his head? Did he have a scheme for their escape, or would he let the kidnappers negotiate with her father? He appeared so realxed that her doubts flooded back. Perhaps he was in league with these men, and Parek's threat to kill him had been a cover-up to protect him! If she didn't let on she understood Teleguayan, they might say something to give her a clue.

'I can understand you wanting to kidnap me.' Her voice betrayed no sign of nerves. 'But there's no reason for you to hold my chauffeur.'

Parek laughed. 'How concerned you are for Mark! Perhaps he's been a real guard of your body, eh?'

Charlotte's embarrassment was overshadowed by the shock of hearing Parek refer to him by his first name, but she did her best to hide it. 'I assume you're from Teleguay,' she said. 'So you must know you won't do your political image any good by harming me.'

'Ah, you speak our language, then?'

'No,' she lied. 'But I recognise the sound of it.'

'Then let me assure you we won't harm you—providing your father does as he's told.'

Charlotte shrugged and stared out of the
window. They had left Cannes behind and were
heading inland. She was surprised they hadn't gone
on the motorway, but assumed Parek considered it
dangerous. Motorway entrances and exits were
easy to block off, and if these men feared capture
they stood a better chance of escape on a minor
road.

'How did you know I'd be at the gallery?' she
asked Parek.

'We've been following you for months, waiting
till General Vargar was in power before we
kidnapped you. Borra and Lucca made friends
with your artist in St-Paul and found out you were
searching for a gallery. We knew the Rosalia was
for sale and obtained the keys to it. The rest you
know.'

'Where are you taking us?'

'To——'

Gizzer interrupted in a spate of angry
Teleguayan, warning Parek to keep his mouth
shut. There was a sharp exchange between the two,
and Gizzer lapsed into silence. It confirmed
Charlotte's belief that Parek was in charge, though
if anything befell him it was clear that Gizzer
would take over. The thought was unnerving.

They reached a crossroads and drove for several
miles along a minor road before stopping in the
shade of a cypress tree.

'Make yourselves comfortable,' Parek
announced. 'We're staying here till late afternoon.'

'Why?' Mark spoke for the first time.

'Because we have to go through a few villages, and it's better if we do so when people are in their homes.'

'You mean we'll be stuck in this car for hours?' Charlotte exclaimed.

'Yes.'

She knew better than to argue, and tried to relax.

With the engine turned off, and consequently no air-conditioning, the heat in the car was unbearable, especially as the windows were kept closed. Occasionally one or other of the men stepped out to stretch his legs, but neither she nor Mark were allowed to.

The hours dragged by and Charlotte, stupefied by the heat, stared out at the landscape. It was scorched by the heat of summer, the sun so intense it had absorbed much of the water, robbing the richness from the red-brown earth and turning it beige, transforming the hedgerows from green to grey. Only the bougainvillaea glowed with purple brilliance.

At last Parek pronounced it safe to resume their journey, and for the next half-hour they drove trhough several mountain villages where, as he had predicted, shutters were already being drawn on the shops. Unlike the tourist areas, closing time here was earlier.

It wasn't until they had left the third village far behind that the Citroën turned down a rutted lane and stopped in front of an old stone farmhouse with narrow windows, grey flagstones and a rose-tiled roof. At any other time Charlotte would have delighted in its rustic simplicity, but now she saw it as her prison.

'Upstairs,' Parek ordered as they entered a square hall. 'I don't think the two of you will object to sharing a room.' He pushed past to open a door into a small bedroom furnished with two wooden chairs and a rickety single bed.

'I want a room of my own,' she demanded instantly.

'This isn't a hotel.'

'Parek's right,' Mark said. 'Don't make a fuss, Miss Beauville.'

Charlotte rounded on him. 'Which the hell side are *you* on?'

'The side of reason. So stop making a fuss.'

For several seconds she didn't trust herself to speak. 'When are you contacting my father?' she finally asked Parek.

'As soon as we can. If he does as he's told, you'll be home in a few days.'

'Why not tomorrow?'

'Because your father will have to prepare and sign binding documents giving our government all his assets in our country. So curb your impatience and make yourself at home with your faithful retainer!'

With a mocking laugh he went out and locked the door, leaving Charlotte staring at the lean-faced man in front of her, and wondering whether she was closeted with a friend or a foe.

CHAPTER TWELVE

ONLY when Parek's steps died away did Charlotte speak to Mark. 'Well, what plans do you have for getting us out of here?'

'None. I may be paid to watch over you, but there isn't enough money in the world to make me risk my life saving you.'

'You swine!'

'I'm sorry you don't like the truth.'

As he spoke, he motioned her to silence and pointed to the door, miming to show he thought someone who listening outside. 'Take it easy and watch your tongue,' he said aloud. 'As Parek told you, if your father has any sense you'll be free in a few days.'

A floorboard creaked outside and he tiptoed to the door and pressed his ear to it. A few seconds went by before he straightened and nodded. 'They've gone,' he mouthed. 'But I suggest we keep our voices down.'

'How do you know they've gone?' she whispered. 'Why didn't you peep through the keyhole?'

'And stare directly into another eye?' He gave a grim smile. 'I might defer to you in social matters, but you'll have to take my advice when dealing with the Pareks of this world.'

'How knowledgeable you sound! But then you're a man of many parts, aren't you? Which reminds me, how did Parek know your name?'

'He's been keeping watch on us for weeks—you heard him say so. He probably knows as much about me as he does of you.'

'I dare say he knows *more* about you than I do,' she rejoined.

Ignoring this, Mark went to the window and Charlotte collapsed on a chair, her brave façade of the last few hours crumbling. 'If I hadn't left the villa without you, none of this would have occurred.'

'Unfortunately I can't agree with you. Even if I'd been with you from the start, the end result would have been the same. I'm at fault for not checking everyone you arranged to see. It's possible Lebrun—the painter—was in on the plot. Who gave you his name?'

'Lila.'

'Hmm. I can't see her helping the rebels! I guess Parek was telling the truth about Borra and Luca following you to Lebrun's studio and then pumping him for information.'

'What are our chances of escaping?'

'Not good.'

'Can't we climb on to the roof and——'

'We have to get out of the window first, and they'd spot us.'

'So we stay here like sitting ducks?'

'It's better than being dead ones! The best thing

you can do is relax. Why not lie down?'

'I'm too hungry to relax. It's hours since I've eaten.'

'We're bound to be fed soon. It isn't in their interest to starve you. Which reminds me—thanks for stopping Parek from shooting me.'

'I didn't do it for your sake,' she retorted. 'I'm hoping you'll be more useful to me alive than dead.'

'Whatever your motives,' came the dry answer, 'I owe you my life.'

She shrugged and peered at herself in the fly-blown mirror hanging on the wall in front of her. In her pale lemon dress she was like a jonquil. Her flaming hair glowed, appearing even richer in this dim, lacklustre room.

Footsteps approached, a key turned and Borra entered with a tray. He set it on the wooden table by the window and stomped out, locking the door behind him.

Charlotte peered at the dishes. 'Soup and bread,' she muttered. 'Do you think we'll get anything else?'

'I doubt it. Have it while it's hot. It smells good.'

'That's a lie if ever I heard one! But I'm too hungry to care.' She ate quickly without tasting it, then set her empty plate on the tray. 'I wish I had a toothbrush.'

'Salt on your finger is a good substitute,' Mark informed her. 'I'll hang on to the salt cellar.'

She sighed. 'Do they honestly expect my father

to give up everything he owns in Teleguay?'

'Yes. They'll also ask him to issue a statement saying he supports the new regime. They believe that if he does that, other big corporations will follow suit, which will force the Western powers to recognise General Vargar.'

'Dad will never give in to the rebels.'

'He has no choice if he wants you back.'

From beneath her lashes, Charlotte studied Mark. Funny, but she could no longer think of him as Rayner. It was obviously connected with his declaration of love. Love? she thought sourly. Expediency, more likely. After all, even if he were in cahoots with Parek, the Beauville billions might be incentive enough for him to forgo his political beliefs. Well, here was her chance to put him to the test.

'I don't think my father will give in as easily as you assume,' she said. 'He may wait to see if you can get us out.'

'I hope he won't wait too long! We don't stand a chance of escaping. Lucca's positioned outside, and Borra brings him his food, which means they're keeping constant watch on us.'

'You know so much about their intentions, maybe you're in league with them!'

Mark's chuckle was faintly mocking. 'Sorry to disappoint you, but I'm an ordinary bloke doing a job I like best—taking care of the rich and living like one of them!'

Charlotte's temper boiled over. 'Which was the reason for your declaration of love, I suppose?'

'Oh, no,' he said gently. 'I meant that.'

'Why should I believe you?'

'Why should I put myself in your power?'

She frowned. 'My power?'

'Admitting how I feel makes me vulnerable with you. You can hurt me very much, if you want to.'

'I could only do that if you genuinely loved me.'

Yet, even if he didn't, she knew she wouldn't wish to hurt him. Her eyes ranged over his neat, composed features, the silky brown hair that curled ever so slightly despite its rigorous brushing, the smoke-grey eyes that stared back at her, yet disclosed nothing of the inner man. Oh, lord, if only she knew if he were honest or a liar.

Trembling, she turned away. 'Isn't there the slightest chance of our escaping?'

'We might make it if we were near a town,' he replied. 'But even if we got out of here undetected—which I can't see us doing—they'd discover we'd gone long before we reached civilisation.'

'Perhaps there's another farm nearby?'

'I didn't see one.'

'How spineless you are!'

If she had hoped to spark off his temper, she failed, for he merely smiled. 'I prefer to call myself a realist. We aren't in a James Bond film. The bullets here are for real, and when you're dead there's no getting up from the floor when the cameras stop turning. If I put you at risk, your father would be furious, and justifiably so. Our best bet is to sit tight. Once your father is assured you'll be unharmed, he——'

'You think they might kill me even if he does as they ask?'

'Not as long as Parek's in charge,' Mark said. 'It's the others I'm not sure of.'

'You're frightening me on purpose.'

'I'm merely warning you not to try their patience.' He fell silent as Borra returned for the tray. 'Any chance of an extra blanket?' he asked politely. 'You won't want us to freeze to death.'

Borra clumped out, coming back almost at once with a thin grey blanket.

Mark spread it on the bed. It was already dark enough to switch on the light, but the illumination from its naked bulb made their surroundings appear even more dreary, and Charlotte insisted he switch it off. Slowly the purple sky turned to indigo and then black, though they were saved from darkness by the sickle moon.

'I don't know why, but I'm awfully tired,' she sighed.

'It's stress. Lie down and try to sleep.'

Docilely she slipped off her shoes and lay on the bed.

'Get under the blanket,' he suggested. 'It's clean enough.'

Again she obeyed him and covered herself to her chin. She tensed, waiting to see what he intended doing, but he settled himself on a chair and put his feet on the other one.

'You can't sleep like that,' she said, irritated to find her voice shaky. 'You'd better come on the bed.'

'I'm fine here.'

'Don't be silly. At least we can be civilised about this.'

Silently he rose and came to lie beside her, but above the blanket. He was careful not to touch her, and the racing of her heart settled to a steady beat.

'You'll get cold,' she whispered after a short while. 'Cover yourself with the blanket.'

He did so, still silent, and careful to keep as much distance from her as possible, though Charlotte gradually became aware of the warmth of him. How motionless he was, how quiet. Inexplicably it made her conscious of his strength, the power he kept leashed. He would make a dangerous enemy, and she wished she knew if he would also make a loyal friend. Suddenly petrified of what might happen to her, she clutched at him.

'I don't want to die! Not here, not like this.'

'You won't die, Miss Beauville. We'll get out of this alive.'

'How can you be sure?'

'Because General Vargar won't want to be held responsible for your death.'

'I see.' She closed her eyes, then almost at once opened them.

'It's silly for you to go on calling me Miss Beauville when we're stuck in the same room like this and——'

'Very well,' he interrupted her. 'Now be quiet and sleep.'

'I'm too frightened. It's horrible to know people can hate me because of my father's position.'

'No one hates you,' Mark said in a thick voice, and gathered her close.

Nestling in his arms, Charlotte experienced a sense of homecoming, and couldn't believe he would ever harm her. 'I'm glad you're with me, Mark.'

'So am I.'

His breath was warm on her hair and, though she knew she was courting danger, she desperately wanted him to kiss her. She raised her head until their mouths were almost touching.

'Don't,' he said in a strangled voice. 'There's a limit even to *my* control.'

'Only a kiss,' she pleaded.

With a sigh, he lowered his lips to hers. They were firm and cool, and she knew he had no intention of making them otherwise. But she wasn't going to accept this. She had been fighting her attraction to him from the beginning, and now they were in this fraught situation she couldn't fight any longer. All that mattered was that he loved her, and in his arms she felt a complete woman.

Her lips parted and her tongue delicately stroked his lower lip. But his mouth remained closed and she gave it a little nip. 'Kiss me properly,' she breathed, and lightly touched his body.

He jerked back as though her touch were fire, then with an incoherent exclamation pressed her flat on the mattress and straddled her. His mouth sought hers and his tongue penetrated the warm depth. Gone was his hesitation, his holding back. He was afire with passion and he had to assuage it. Groaning deep in his throat, he drank her moistness, his tongue probing, demanding a response she was eager to give.

Whimpering in ecstasy, she reared her body to meet his, glorying in the heavy pressure of him on her breasts, her belly; the weight of his swollen erection on her thigh.

'No!' The cry came from deep inside him, and he pushed her roughly away and turned on his side. 'Charlotte, don't! You're overwrought, not thinking straight. I can't take advantage . . .'

'I want you,' she whispered, clinging to him.

'I know. And I want you. But not like this. When you give yourself to me I want it to be in freedom, not because you're scared and I'm the only one you can rely on.'

He was right, of course, and she loved him for caring for her enough to let understanding curb his passion. Sliding close, she curved herself into his back.

'Dear Mark, I do trust you.'

'Good.' He sounded pleased, yet he was still taut and did not turn to face her. 'Sleep well, my love.'

Closing her eyes, she breathed him in, marvelling that in this dingy room, hungry, unwashed, she had come nearer to total joy than at any time in her life.

CHAPTER THIRTEEN

MARK awoke with the dawn, and turned his head to regard the girl beside him.

Charlotte was still asleep, her hair tumbled round her face, her skin flushed. Never had he seen her look as lovely or as vulnerable as she did now. Her lashes were like dark half-moons on her cheeks, and her lips were slightly parted. As if aware of being watched, she stirred but did not waken, and he eased himself carefully off the bed so as not to disturb her, and crept over to the window.

Gizzer had taken over the watch and was leaning against the gate, playing idly with his rifle, as though he enjoyed the feel of it. The man was a killer and had to be watched. A sound behind him made him stiffen, and he turned as the door opened.

Parek stood on the threshold, glancing from Charlotte's sleeping form to Mark. He leered meaningfully, then beckoned him into the passage. 'We haven't managed to talk to Beauville,' he grunted. 'When we phoned the house yesterday, he had left for New York.'

Mark wasn't surprised. In the short time he had been at the villa, the man had been to the States

twice, Tokyo and Sydney once, and had chaired
meetings in London, Oslo and Paris on one and the
same day! 'He has a phone in his jet,' he
murmured.

'It's too easy to trace the origin of a satellite
call,' Parek said. 'We left word we have his
daughter and will be contacting him later this
morning. That should bring him running.' The
small brown eyes were mocking. 'If I'd hired you
to watch over a daughter of mine, and she'd been
taken hostage, you wouldn't live long once I found
you!'

'I wasn't very good, was I?' Mark agreed, then
said, 'I'd like to talk to you.'

'So talk.'

'Not here. In private.'

Parek led the way down to the kitchen at the rear
of the house. A large, discoloured china sink and
wooden draining-board took up one wall, while
against the smaller stood a blackened Calor gas
cooker. A narrow window overlooked the back
garden, where the grass was almost waist high.
Parek filled a tin kettle and set it on a flame.

'Be quick, Englishman. I'm not happy having
you down here.'

'I won't make a run for it. I believe in your
cause.'

'Yeah? Is that why you were guarding the
heiress?'

'It got me into the household, didn't it? You
aren't the only one who wants the girl. My
organisation does, too. Beauville controls too

many British companies and we intend making sure he eases his grip.'

Parek spooned coffee into two mugs and added hot water; all this in silence, his face a mask. '*You* were going to kidnap her?'

'Yes. Our people have been planning it for months. But you beat us to it. Another twenty-four hours and we'd have had her.'

Parek sipped noisily from his mug. 'What's your group called?'

'PTP—Power to the People.'

'I've never heard of it.'

Mark straddled a chair and sipped his coffee. 'How many had heard of General Vargar before the uprising?'

'That's true,' Parek agreed. 'Are you the leader?'

Mark pulled a wry face. 'You kidding? My leaders are rich and powerful. Bosses on the surface, but working against them underground.' Parek's grin showed he found the idea appealing, and Mark pressed home his advantage. 'I'll give you a number to call in London. They'll confirm what I've told you.'

'Sorry, Englishman, we always work alone.'

Mark set down his mug. 'Why can't we both get something out of this? Contact London and——'

'No, I don't trust you.'

'Don't trust who?' Gizzer demanded, stepping into the kitchen. 'What's *he* doing here?' A thumb indicated Mark.

'Talking to me,' Parek grunted. 'And don't

question my authority.'

'When my life's at stake, I'll question anyone.'

Speaking in his own language, Parek put the other man in the picture.

'He's lying!' Gizzer exploded in English, wanting Mark to understand what was said. 'Get rid of him now.'

'I'm sorry you disbelieve me,' Mark put in. 'If we'd got the girl first, we'd have tried to help *you*.'

'How would you have got her?' Gizzer sneered.

'I've been teaching her to water-ski in the bay. This afternoon another speed-boat would have been waiting for us half a mile out. By now, we'd have been in Morocco.' Mark spoke directly to Parek. 'When Beauville's agreed to your demands, let *us* have her.'

Gizzer gave a girlish, high-pitched laugh. 'When we've finished with her she won't be worth having!'

It required an immense effort for Mark not to thump his fist into the man's face. 'I thought you weren't going to harm her.'

'We won't,' Parek stated emphatically.

'More fool you,' Gizzer grunted.

The two men glared at each other and the younger one backed down. But Mark knew the tension would explode more violently next time. He felt drained of energy. He had played his ace and lost. Unless he came up with something else, he and Charlotte were doomed. Yet perhaps there *was* another card to play.

Laconically he rose. 'If I put my hand down the

inside of my trousers and bring out a gun, will you please not shoot me?'

Parek stared at him dumbfounded. 'We took your gun away.'

'Watch.' Slowly Mark lowered his hand down the inside of his trousers and drew it out again, a small but lethal gun in his fingers. Carefully he set it on the table. 'If I'd been lying to you, Parek, I could have shot you while we were alone in here. It has a silencer, so no one would have heard. Then I'd have killed the two men upstairs and come back to finish off Gizzer.' He had in fact considered doing it, but had been worried lest it went wrong. 'I could have killed the four of you,' he repeated, and snapped his fingers. 'Just like that.'

Parek blanched, then swung round on his compatriot. 'Well, do you still think he's lying?'

'Who knows?' Gizzer was clearly disconcerted. 'But it makes no difference. I wouldn't let his organisation use the girl.'

Parek spoke to Mark. 'Gizzer's right. I'm glad you told us the truth, but you must remain upstairs.'

Mark went to the door. 'I voluntarily gave you my gun. Please remember that.'

Wondering if the gesture had been futile or if it might yet bear fruit, Mark returned to the bedroom.

CHAPTER FOURTEEN

CHARLOTTE opened her eyes and studied the ceiling, puzzled to see it was dingy grey and peeling. What on earth . . .? Memory returned, and with a cry she sat up and looked for Mark.

He wasn't there! She was alone.

Petrified, she ran to the door. It was unlocked, but as she went to open it she drew back, remembering he had warned her she would put her life in jeopardy if she tried to escape. But where was he? Had Parek shot him, after all?

The pain that wrenched through her was so intense, she collapsed on the bed. At last she faced the truth and admitted how childish her pretences had been. She loved Mark! Regardless of his background, uncaring whether her wealth was of prime interest to him, she would become his wife. He had never kow-towed to her, never been intimidated by her position, and, though she had desperately tried to bring him to heel, he had remained his own man. Oh, he had put on a humble act, but she had always known it *was* an act, and that beneath it he was strong, determined and unwilling to bend the knee to anyone.

But she no longer had the chance to tell him how deeply she cared, and sobs racked her as she cried for a life destroyed, and her own life which, from now on, would never be totally fulfilled.

Strong arms grasped her and she screamed and tried to wrench free.

'Charlotte, be still! It's me.'

With a gasp she turned and saw Mark. 'I thought you were dead!' she cried. 'When I awoke and found you gone, I——'

'I'm fine,' he assured her. 'I wanted to talk to Parek and we went downstairs. I was trying to find out if they'd spoken to your father. But he flew to New York yesterday—before he knew we hadn't returned to the villa for lunch.'

'I bet he flew back immediately he knew I was missing,' Charlotte said. 'When is Parek calling him again?'

'This morning.'

Her comment was forestalled by the arrival of their breakfast: coffee, half a stale *baguette*, and a saucer full of apricot jam.

She poured two mugs of coffee and handed one to Mark, then broke off a piece of the bread, leaving the larger hunk for him. He took it, divided it again and gave her another piece.

'Share and share alike,' he said calmly.

His gesture was her undoing, and with a sob she knelt at his side. 'I've been so blind about you, Mark.'

'Have you?'

'You know I have. I've loved you almost from the beginning, but I wouldn't admit it. Then this morning—when I thought you'd been shot—I saw how stupid I'd been. I don't care if you do love my money more than me! You're still the only man I want.'

'That's a back-handed compliment if ever I heard one!'

'I didn't think you'd want me to lie. I know you find me sexy, but I won't fool myself you'd have said what you did in the gallery yesterday if I were poor.'

'How right you are!'

His swift admission shattered her, but she tried to hide it.

'If you'd been poor,' he went on, 'I'd have asked you to marry me a week after meeting you! It was your damn money that held me back.' He hauled her up and into his arms. 'I know all the doubts you have about me, but I do care for you. More than I ever thought it possible to care for anyone.'

Tilting her chin, he fastened his mouth on hers. Mark had kissed her with anger and with passion, but never with such tenderness. Feeling like a flower warmed by the sun, she opened her lips to him. With deliberate slowness his tongue slid into her mouth and moved sinuously against hers. Responding to its touch, she absorbed the taste of him, growing heady with the sharp stirring of passion.

With a moan she clasped his neck and ran her fingers through the silky hair that lay on his nape. At her touch, the gentleness left him and he crushed her hard against his body, shaping the soft curve of her stomach to his strongly muscled one, the burgeoning swell of her breasts to the rock-hard wall of his chest. His tongue went wild inside her, darting deep and draining her sweetness before he withdrew it and lowered his head to place his lips around the jutting nipples that his wandering hands had aroused to sharp peaks.

As he suckled the swollen buds, a ribbon of desire lanced from her breasts to the fiery core between her loins. With a sob she thrust her thighs forward, parting her legs to twine one around his and press the aching nub upon the tumescent muscle throbbing against her stomach.

He shuddered, and with a hoarse cry pushed her away. But it was only to find her burning warmth with his fingers. Gently he rubbed her, his touch growing fiercer as she writhed wildly, shaken by an ecstasy she couldn't control. Then his mouth was on hers again, his other hand clasping her buttocks and pulling her hard upon him so that his finger penetrated deeper inside her, stroking, massaging, rubbing backwards and forwards until she gave a shuddering cry and splintered into a thousand mindless raptures.

Exhausted, she slumped forward, but his arms supported her as he drew her on to the bed and cradled her in his lap. Strangely shy, it was impossible to meet his eyes, and she burrowed into his chest.

'Darling girl,' he said huskily. 'Why won't you look at me?'

'I—I can't.' She moistened her lips. 'You've

seen what you do to me—yet you didn't—you never . . .'

'Because I want to take my time with you,' he whispered into her hair. 'I want to absorb you into my bones, savour the taste and scent of you, fill you with my seed until you're bursting.' His voice thickened and he clasped her closer. 'Now isn't the time or place for hours of loving, and until it is, I have to keep my self-control.'

'Why did you let me lose mine?'

'To destroy your doubts of me, and show you how it's going to be between us. If I start making love to you, it will be hours before I can think straight, and I need all my wits to try to get us out of here alive.'

His answer was everything she had hoped for, and her embarrassment disappeared. 'I can't wait to see Dad's face when I tell him I'm going to marry you!' She stopped as she felt Mark stiffen. 'What is it? You do want to marry me, don't you?'

'I was just getting round to proposing,' he said unsteadily. 'But you floored me by getting in first.'

'You'll have to be on your toes to keep pace with the Beauvilles!' she teased, then with a change of mood said earnestly, 'Don't ever lie to me, Mark. If you don't want marriage, say so.'

'Don't want it? It's what I've wanted since I set eyes on you. To know that we belong to each other, that I can love you and cherish you with my life.'

Anguish darkened his eyes and, knowing the cause of it, she placed her hand over his lips.

'Don't blame yourself because we were taken hostage. It was more my fault than yours. I provoked you so much that you weren't thinking straight.'

'I'm paid to think straight. I'll never forgive myself for not doing so.'

'You must. I don't want a guilt-ridden husband!' Seeing he was still distressed, she changed the subject. 'What will you do when we're married? You aren't the sort to be idle.'

'I'll be your unpaid protector,' he said lightly.

'I take that for granted. But I'm talking about a job. Do you fancy running the gallery with me?'

'Not my scene.'

'Does working for my father appeal? He's always hoped I'll marry someone he can train to take over from him when he retires.'

'I don't think I'd be capable of stepping into his shoes,' Mark said. 'Perhaps there's something else I can do in his organisation. Missions requiring diplomacy, or things of that sort.'

'I can certainly vouch for your diplomacy!' she giggled. 'Without even trying, you had me eating out of your hand.'

'When you weren't biting it!' He knuckled her chin. 'For the moment, let's put the future on the slow burner and concentrate on the present.'

Charlotte sobered. 'When I found you gone this morning, I also discovered the door had been left unlocked.'

'Why didn't you try to escape?'

'You said we were too isolated to get away with

it.'

'I've changed my mind. If you get another chance, go.'

'Not without you.'

'Forget me,' he insisted. 'You're the one in danger. With you free, I can take care of myself.' He pressed her arm warningly as Borra unlocked the door and beckoned him.

'You're wanted downstairs,' he grunted. 'Not you,' he said as Charlotte went to follow.

'Do you object if I go to the bathroom?' she asked icily.

He waited for her to enter it, then locked her in, mumbling that she should shout when she wanted to be let out.

To her amazement the narrow window was open. Last time she had been in here it had been bolted down. She peered out, longing to breathe fresh air, and felt excitement grip her as she came face to face with an olive tree.

A tree! On tiptoe she craned for a better view of it. It was gnarled and old, the trunk thick and the branches solid. Solid enough to support her weight! Her heart thumped erratically. Dared she make a break for it? Leave Mark, as he had urged her to do if she had the chance? The thought of deserting him filled her with shame, yet he had been so insistent that she knew she had to obey him.

Without further ado she levered herself on to the window-ledge and began squeezing through it. A thick branch was almost touching the wall of the farmhouse, and she stretched out her leg and found a foothold on it.

Charlotte had not had the sort of childhood where she had roamed free and climbed trees, and she felt an unusual sense of trepidation as she felt the bough swing beneath her weight. Biting back a gasp, she clung to it, her hold only relaxing as it gradually ceased moving. Heavens, what was wrong with her? She'd been further from the ground on a diving-board than she was here, and there was no reason to be uptight. Slightly more confident, she eased forward, seeking another foothold on a lower branch. A thin, twiggy stem tangled in her hair and she stifled a cry of pain. If only she'd had the sense to plait it and wind it round her head. Carefully she prised the strands loose, grimacing as several red-gold hairs were lost. Free again, she continued her descent, careful to choose the thickest, leafiest boughs in order to remain hidden as long as possible.

Clinging to the next branch down, she peeped through a cluster of leaves and had her first clear view of the garden. Panic ripped through her. Parek was only a few yards distant, chatting to Mark. Damn! She'd thought they were in the kitchen. Mouth dry as an old bone, she eased back, waiting. In her bright yellow dress she was as obvious as a sunflower in an onion patch! If Parek glanced up, he'd spot her instantly. Sweat trickled down her forehead and into her eyes, but she dared not move to wipe it away. The seconds ticked by, each as long as a minute. She couldn't stay here much longer. Her arms were aching from holding on to the branch, and cramp was threatening her calf muscles.

She was debating the feasibility of climbing back to the bathroom, when Parek laughed and swung round, gripping Mark's arm as he moved with him towards the rear boundary of the garden. What luck! Her spirits rose and she cautiously lowered herself to the next bough. It swayed menacingly and she prayed it wouldn't crack. But, oh, how it creaked! Motionless as a lizard in the sun, she waited for it to settle, then eased along it to the trunk. There was no time to search for footholds and she slithered down it, the rough bark rasping her palms and legs.

Wincing with pain, she lay flat in the tall grass. Parek still had his back to her, and, though Mark was facing her, she wasn't certain if he had seen her. She heard the Teleguayan laugh again, and Mark joined in, making her wonder what had been said.

Pushing it from her mind, she concentrated on the task ahead. A thick hedge stood a short distance to her left, and she cautiously inched towards it. She had no idea what lay beyond. It might be a field or a lane, but she was in no position to be choosy.

'There's Gizzer,' Parek said, and Charlotte flattened herself on the earth, hardly daring to breathe. Nothing happened and she counted to twenty, then carefully turned her head. There was no sign of the man, and she continued to crawl towards the hedge. Another few yards and she would make it!

'There's the girl!' Mark shouted, and Charlotte stopped, paralysed with shock. Mark had given her away! It was impossible! But he had, as he proved by dashing forward and throwing himself on her. Stunned by his perfidy, she lay beneath him, earth filling her mouth and nostrils, but the bile of disgust filling her throat.

Mark was one of *them*.

'For pete's sake,' he muttered in her ear, 'you could have been shot!'

Giving her no chance to reply, he lifted himself from her and hauled her to her feet as the two Teleguayans reached their side.

'You've got excellent eyesight, my friend,' Parek said.

'Luckily for you,' Mark grunted. 'Otherwise she'd have escaped.'

'Not from me,' Gizzer grated, fondling his gun as if it were a woman. 'Another few seconds and I'd have seen her, too.' His dead eyes ran over her. 'Try it again, rich bitch, and you won't live to tell the tale.'

'Come,' Mark said, giving her a rough shake. 'I'll take you upstairs.'

Parek scanned the open bathroom window. 'From now on you won't be left on your own,' he shouted after her. 'You're a fool to put your life at risk. What does a few more days matter to you?'

None too gently, Mark hauled Charlotte round the house to the front door and upstairs. He didn't speak until they were alone in the room.

'You were damn lucky I saw you!' he whispered savagely. 'If I hadn't, you'd have been killed.'

'Or free!' she flared. 'You stopped me. You stopped me!'

'Gizzer was coming round the side of the house with his gun. You heard him say so. Another few steps and he'd have seen you and shot you!'

'He had to say that,' she cried. 'If he hadn't, he'd have seemed as big a fool as Parek. How *could* you have given me away?'

'It was for your own safety.' Mark kept his voice low. 'Can't you see that?'

'Hey, Englishman!' Borra's head came round the door. 'Parek says you don't have to stay with the girl. You can come and sit with us.'

'Thanks.' Mark smiled.

Charlotte put the distance of the room between them. For a brief moment she had almost believed his behaviour in the garden had been prompted by fear for her safety, but now she knew better.

'You're in league with them! I was right about you, after all.' She trembled with bitterness. 'No wonder you knew where to find me in Cannes.'

'Don't be an idiot! I didn't even know the name of the gallery. It was pure luck I saw your car.'

'It had nothing to do with luck. You're a traitor! Go down to your friends and stay there,' she said contemptuously. 'I never want to see you again.'

CHAPTER FIFTEEN

MISERY robbed Charlotte of all strength, and she
sank on to the bed and buried her face in her
hands. She despised Mark, yet loathed herself even
more for loving him.

His sudden return shocked her, and she looked
at him with loathing. 'Get out!' she exploded.

Ignoring her, he came to her side. 'Don't judge
me, Charlotte.' His voice was low, almost
menacing. 'You don't know the facts.'

'I know enough to hate you!' Her hands clawed
out wildly, but he caught them and dragged them
down to her sides.

'Control yourself!' he bit out. 'I only came to
tell you Parek's gone to telephone your father.'

'Thanks. Now get——' She stopped as she heard
a car racing down the lane, and darted across the
window in time to see a dusty black Fiat draw to a
stop.

'It's Gizzer,' Mark said behind her. 'That's odd.
He was supposed to be driving behind Parek to
keep watch while he telephoned.'

A high-pitched moan—as of an animal in
pain—came from downstairs, and Charlotte
trembled. 'What was that?'

'I'm going to find out.'

As the door closed behind Mark there was another cry from below, and Charlotte was convinced something terrible had occurred.

Mark's return, his face pale, confirmed it, and she took an involuntary step towards him. 'What's wrong?'

'Parek's hurt—a broken leg and concussion—and Gizzer brought him back.'

'You mean my father——'

'No, no, nothing to do with your father. Parek didn't even get to call him. He crashed the Citroën into an ox-cart half a mile down the road. Gizzer couldn't take him to hospital in case your father had notified the police you've been taken hostage, so he brought him back here.'

'Does that mean Gizzer's in control?'

'I'm afraid so.' Mark's eyebrows drew together in a dark line. 'Once your father's signed over his assets in Teleguay, Gizzer will kill you.'

'Why?'

'For pleasure. You represent everything he hates, and I do mean hate.' Mark peered through the window. 'Nobody's on watch in the garden, so they must all be with Parek. It looks as if now is our chance to get out.'

She swallowed hard. 'You're going to help me escape?'

'Myself, too. It has to be the bathroom window again. We daren't risk the stairs.'

'I won't go. You're trying to kill me! You'll make it seem you had to shoot me while I was escaping.'

'Are you crazy? Why should I want to kill you?'

'Because once I'm free I'll denounce you for what you are!'

'Keep your voice down,' he grated, 'or we'll *both* be shot.'

'Not *you*?'

'Oh, yes, very much me. Gizzer's no friend of mine.'

'Is he worried you might take over from him?' she sneered. Mark's reason for wanting to escape was clear: it wasn't fear for *her* safety, but his own!

Without replying, he dragged her to the door and opened it gingerly. Putting a warning finger to his lips, he tiptoed with her to the bathroom. A few fraught minutes later, they slithered down the olive tree to the ground.

'Keep low,' he whispered. 'One of the men may be looking through the kitchen window.'

Charlotte bent double as she crawled after Mark. The grass was filled with droning insects, and twice she had to stop herself sneezing. After what seemed an eternity they reached the hedge.

'It's quicker to go over the top,' he advised, 'but safer to keep close to the ground and crawl through it. Let's find a gap.'

They inched their way along the hedge until they reached a bush with sparser leaves than its neighbours. Wriggling through, they found themselves in a narrow country lane.

'We can straighten now,' Mark said, 'but we must run for it. Any minute one of them may check our room.'

'Is it wise to keep to the lane?' Charlotte questioned. 'This is where they'll look for us first.'

'I know. But it's the fastest route away from here.'

Catching her by the hand, Mark began running. The rutted path seemed never-ending, and she had a sharp stitch in her side by the time they reached a secondary road.

'What do we do now?' she panted.

'See if we can get a lift into Grasse. It's the nearest town.'

'What's wrong with the village?'

'It's the first place Gizzer will head for.'

Charlotte shivered and glanced round, but the lane was deserted. Suddenly, with a jerk that nearly pulled her arm out of its socket, Mark dragged her backwards through the tall grass bordering the roadside. Even as she went to protest, she heard the low hum of a car. Hardly daring to breathe, they lay flat against the earth, her heart thumping so loudly in her ears that it drowned out the sound of the engine, and all she was conscious of was crippling fear.

'That was the Fiat,' Mark commented. 'Lucky I recognised the sound of the engine.'

'They won't go far without doubling back on their tracks,' Charlotte replied, scrambling to her feet.

'I agree. So we'll change direction and make for the mountains instead of the coast. They won't expect that.'

'Yes, they will. When Gizzer's gone another

kilometre without seeing us, he'll guess we've taken an unexpected direction. You're clever and cunning, Mark, and he knows it as well as I do.'

Mark grinned. 'You're dead right. So I *won't* be cunning, and we won't go up *or* down, but across! This is a war game, Charlotte. It's victory or defeat.'

Cognisance of what defeat meant gave her the strength to keep pace with him as they raced across field after field, sticking as close as possible to the hedgerows. After what seemed hours she had another stitch in her side and a red mist in front of her eyes, making it difficult for her to see.

'I can't breathe,' she cried, and collapsed on to the soft earth. 'Go on without me. I'll burrow under the hedge and——'

'You can't give in now!' Mark dragged her to her feet. 'We go on together or we both stay here.'

'I can't move another step,' she gasped, her legs buckling again.

Silently Mark scooped her into his arms and set off.

Held close to him, she heard the fierce pounding of his heart in her ear, and was painfully aware of the life force in him, a life which Gizzer's bullet could destroy. Tears filled her eyes and she blinked rapidly. Regardless of Mark's treachery, she loved him and would never be able to forget him.

'I think I can walk now,' she ventured. 'I feel better.'

He set her down, then paused to draw breath. 'These fields must belong to a farmer. With any luck we'll soon come to his house.'

'Don't bank on it. In this area the farmer might live in the nearest village.'

'Let's hope you're wrong.' Mark forged on, setting a brisk pace for a hundred yards before abruptly stopping and pointing through a clump of trees to a grey stone house, outside of which stood a dilapidated Renault. 'There's even transport,' he crowed, 'but no phone or electricity.'

'How can you tell?'

'I can't see any wires. They're usually above ground in rural areas.'

'You know a lot about many things,' she taunted. 'I suppose that comes from being all things to all men.'

He ignored her remark. 'Wait here and lie low. Gizzer may know of this farm and put in one of his men as a look-out. He's astute enough to think of everything.'

'So are you.'

'You'd better pray I am,' he said grimly. 'Your life depends on it.'

'Yours, too. And if you get me out of this alive, you'll be a hero.'

To her chagrin he laughed. 'I hadn't thought of that before. But now you mention it, it sounds good.'

'Haven't you any shame?' she cried.

'Absolutely not!'

Motioning her to remain where she was, he moved stealthily towards the house. Charlotte lay on the sweet-smelling earth and tried not to think what would happen if one of the terrorists spotted either of them. Her imagination was still playing havoc with her when Mark returned, panting from the exertion of running.

'It's fine,' he gasped. 'An old couple live there, and the man's agreed to drive us to Grasse. I explained our car had broken down, and that we'd taken a short cut and got lost.'

'Why didn't you tell him the truth?'

'He might have been scared to drive us. Hurry,' he ordered. 'We must get moving.'

The farmer was a garrulous octogenarian who rattled on as much as his Renault as they chugged down the country lanes.

'We should really be lying low in the back,' Mark muttered as the car slowed at a crossing.

'Then why don't we?'

'How do we explain it? Our friendly farmer will either think we're off our rockers, or else get the wind up and turf us out. So watch for the Citroën. If you see it, duck!

Nervously she kept her eyes on the road, though as they reached a long, straight stretch with no other vehicles in sight she relaxed and let her gaze wander to Mark. Never had he appeared more handsome. Their precipitate dash across the countryside had brought added colour to his face, and his rumpled hair and torn shirt intensified his masculine vitality. His hands, those beautifully shaped hands which had held and caressed her, sported long scratches and dried blood, evidence of his clearing a path for her as they had crawled through the hedge. She longed to hold them, draw them to her breast, lick away the blood . . . Dismayed by the tenderness she felt for him, she tore her eyes away and concentrated on the road.

They reached Grasse without incident, and Mark asked the old man to stop at the base of the hill that led to the town. He handed the farmer a fistful of francs and a scrap of paper, then spoke to him in a patois Charlotte didn't understand.

'What did you say to him?' she asked suspiciously as the Renault chugged off.

'I told him you're the daughter of a millionaire and would he call your father and say we were in Grasse and needed help.'

Fear knifed through her. Was he speaking the truth or had he decided he'd been wrong to help her, and was switching sides again? Perhaps he'd asked the man to contact Gizzer?

'I'm not lying,' he stated, as if guessing her thoughts. Yet the vague look in his eyes did not allay her suspicions.

'What do we do now?' she asked.

'Go to the police station. It's up the hill.'

Charlotte's suspicions increased. 'Why didn't you ask the farmer to take us there?'

'Because he wouldn't have been able to make a fast getaway if Gizzer or his henchmen were waiting nearby. It's easier to assess the situation if we approach on foot.'

'How do you know where the police station is?'

'I have a map showing me where all the stations are in this area.'

'So you could avoid them, I suppose,' she said bitterly. 'If it weren't for Parek's accident, you'd never have helped me escape!'

Not deigning to reply, Mark walked briskly up the hill, keeping close to the high stone wall that bordered one side of the road. Following on his heels, Charlotte was aware what a sight she looked, with her dirt-stained dress and unkempt hair. Several passers-by gawped at her, and she debated whether to stop and ask one of them for help.

As she moved towards a young woman pushing a baby buggy, Mark wheeled round, grasped her hand and pulled her closer.

'Let go of me!' she shouted.

'Not till we're in the police station.'

Convinced he had sensed what she'd intended doing, she was consumed with rage. Maybe he *did* mean to take her back to her father, but he patently intended getting the kudos for it.

Sweat poured down her face, but Mark was pulling her uphill too fast for her to wipe it away. 'Slow down,' she gasped, head spinning.

He stopped dead, but only to flatten her against the stone wall. 'Keep back,' he hissed. 'Lucca's standing on the steps of the police station.'

Terror gripped her. 'Isn't there another one we can go to?'

'Gizzer or Borra is bound to be there. Our best bet is to phone the police from the nearest café. If I remember rightly from my last visit here, there's one round the corner.' Cautiously he inched forward for a better view. 'Damn! Gizzer's sitting at an outside table. We'll have to find another phone.'

'Do you think he has other men posted around the town?' she asked shakily.

'I doubt it. There only seemed to be four of them, and with Parek injured there are only three.'

Charlotte failed to gain any comfort from this. 'We're bound to be spotted if we wander round the streets.'

Mark peered cautiously around the wall again. 'There's a bakery across the road. We'll wait for a van to block Gizzer's view, then make a dash for it.'

As he spoke, a large greengrocer's van laden with crates of vegetables rumbled towards them, and, using it for cover, Mark rushed her across the road. There was a shout behind them and, muttering, 'Gizzer's seen us!' Mark veered towards the alley directly in front of them and pushed her through an open door half-way down it.

Charlotte found herself in the back of a shop, and motioned him to close the door.

'It's safer to leave it open,' he whispered, thrusting her down behind a pile of boxes. 'Then he's more likely to run past it.'

His assumption proved correct, for the sound of running footsteps came nearer and then receded. Mark tiptoed to the entrance to satisfy himself the alley was deserted.

'I'll try to make it to the bakery,' he said.

'Don't leave me alone.'

'You'll be safer here. Keep behind the boxes. I'll

contact the police and tell them where you are.'

Startled, she half rose. 'Aren't you coming back, then?'

'It's too risky. Our tricky trio might spot me. Once I've made the call, I'll stay put till you're rescued.'

'Don't you mean stay in hiding?' she flared. 'Then if Gizzer finds me before the police do, you can make your getaway, but if the police find me instead, you can emerge and be a hero!'

'Clever of you to guess,' he said drily, and with a wave of his hand was gone.

Miserably Charlotte counted the passing seconds. Did Mark intend calling the police, as he had said, or was he searching for Gizzer? Yet that didn't make sense. Why go to the trouble of helping her escape if he planned to hand her back to the Teleguayans? Unless he now felt they didn't stand a chance of escaping and had decided to use her as a bargaining point!

I'll hand over Charlotte Beauville if you spare my life. The words were so clear in her mind, she was overcome with despair. Yet not so overcome that she was going to remain here and fall into Gizzer's lap. Better to take fate in her own hands and try to reach the coast on her own.

On the other hand, perhaps she was judging Mark too harshly. He might genuinely be anxious to help her—even if only to save his own skin! Delivering her safely to her father would obtain his heartfelt gratitude and a huge bonus, providing she didn't disclose how two-faced he had been. But why should she protect him when he deserved to go to prison?

The answer was self-evident, and biting back a sigh she quietly shifted her position. One of her legs had gone numb and she massaged it with her hands, wincing as pins and needles shot through it.

There was a soft rustle behind her and she froze. The rustle came again and she relaxed. It was only a mouse scrabbling at some paper. She tried to envisage it—a little creature with a curly tail and twitching nose—but could think only of a large grey rat with beady eyes and sharp teeth! The noise drew nearer and she prayed for the strength to stay where she was, as Mark had ordered. She clenched her hands, her nails digging so painfully into her palms that she didn't immediately feel something cold and hard digging into the nape of her neck. The hair rose on her scalp and she tensed.

'Don't move,' said Gizzer's expressionless voice, 'or I'll blow your head off.'

Blind terror held her rigid. Mark had ratted on her! Had once more turned his coat and thrown in his lot with the rebels.

'Get up and start walking,' the man ordered. 'Borra's waiting in the Fiat half-way down the hill.'

Charlotte obeyed him, and as they emerged in the alley Gizzer linked his arm through hers. 'We're friends, are we not? A young couple strolling in the sunshine.'

Arm in arm, they walked briskly down the street. Everything looked as it had fifteen minutes ago.

The sky was still brilliant blue, the road congested with vehicles, the café opposite teeming with people. At the bottom of the hill a policeman was controlling the traffic, and cars and lorries were piling up behind each other. It was *l'heure d'affluence*—rush hour.

Muttering irritably, Gizzer edged Charlotte between a bike and a lorry. Their progress was slow—impeded by his continually glancing over his shoulder—as if scared of being pounced on. Had she misjudged Mark, after all? Perhaps he hadn't given her away.

A large truck bore down on them, ignoring the white line to break out of the queue. The man next to the driver wore dark glasses and a cloth cap. He seemed vaguely familiar and she stifled a gasp. It was Mark! He was trying to draw near them and take Gizzer unawares.

The *gendarme* waved his arm and the traffic started moving again. The truck was in the forefront and Gizzer paused in the middle of the road to let it pass. The driver slowed down and signalled for them to cross in front of him. Charlotte tensed. If they stayed where they were, Mark didn't have a hope of taking Gizzer by surprise. He could only do that if the Teleguayan crossed the road with his back to the truck.

'I hate standing in the middle of traffic,' she cried, and lunged forward.

Gizzer was forced to follow and the truck rolled forward, too, its door silently and swiftly opening for Mark to take a flying leap on to Gizzer's shoulders. He went sprawling, and Charlotte, free of his hold, ran hell for leather towards the policeman.

Suddenly there were men in blue everywhere, rushing in from all directions. Some headed for the blue Citroën parked further down the hill, some went to Mark's aid, while others cordoned her off protectively.

'You're safe now, Charlotte.' Mark broke through the blue circle, and only as she felt his hands lifting her did she realise she was crouching down in the gutter.

'S-safe?' she asked, teeth chattering.

'Yes. You'll be home in an hour.'

Never had the word seemed more wonderful. She tried to speak, but no sound came. Mark's face drew nearer and then receded, the sky tilted, the ground rose to meet it, and for the first time in her life Charlotte fainted.

CHAPTER SIXTEEN

MARK didn't accompany Charlotte in the car that was taking her to her father. The last she saw of him he was climbing into a police car, though from the friendly smiles and back-slapping all round he was evidently regarded as a hero. If only they knew! She presumed he had gone to make a statement, and wondered what cock and bull story he would fabricate.

'What will happen to the Teleguayans?' she asked the sergeant beside her.

'They'll be tried and sent to prison. You had a lucky escape, *mademoiselle*.'

She nodded and wearily closed her eyes, not opening them again until they stopped at the lodge gates of the Beauville estate. Within minutes they were at the villa, and she stumbled from the car into her father's waiting arms.

'Thank heaven you're safe!' he exclaimed, tears coursing down his cheeks. 'They didn't hurt you, did they? You weren't given any drugs? If they——'

'I'm fine, Dad.' She smiled valiantly at him, then greeted the staff who were waiting behind him. Most had known her since her childhood, and a few were openly crying.

'I've prepared your favourite lobster thermidor for dinner, Miss Charlotte,' Yvette choked.

Charlotte kissed the plump cheek. 'As soon as I've had a long hot soak I'll be ready for it!'

Yvette bustled off happily, and Maria darted upstairs ahead of Charlotte to run the bath.

Hugging her close, her father went with her to her room, promising to return after she had had a chance to come to herself.

Lying in the warm, scented water, Charlotte's tension flowed away, leaving behind a vacuum that inexorably filled with depression. She had her freedom, but she no longer had Mark. She had known him only a matter of weeks, yet in that time he had been her constant companion, hardly ever out of her sight and, if she were honest, hardly ever out of her thoughts.

But from today she would never willingly see or think of him again. Regardless of what story he concocted for the police and her father, *she* knew the truth, and she was still in two minds whether or not to tell her father and leave him to decide what to do. If she covered up for him, he might do the dirty on someone else!

The idea was so appalling that she jumped out of the bath and reached for her towel. It was morally wrong of her to keep quiet, even if it meant Mark going to prison!

Prison. It was even more appalling to think of him being captive for years, and torn by indecision yet again she paced the room, only stopping as Maria wheeled in a trolley laden with fresh asparagus, the promised lobster thermidor, and a bowl of fresh peaches.

But Charlotte had lost her appetite, and was staring disconsolately at the food when her father walked in.

'You look much better,' he beamed, feasting his eyes on her.

'I feel it,' she lied.

'Good. Mark called me a short while ago from police headquarters in Nice.'

Charlotte's fork clattered to the tray. 'What did he tell you?'

'Everything. How you were abducted from the art gallery, that he was afraid to escape with you in case you were shot, and why he changed his mind when Parek was injured. Thank heavens he did. I'm sure he was right about Gizzer shooting you once I'd given in to their demands.'

'It's all over now, Dad.' Charlotte hugged him close, unhappy at sight of his pallor. 'Forget it.'

'I can't. When I think how nearly I could have lost you . . .' With a shaky hand, he stroked her hair. 'I intend coming to an arrangement with General Vargar over my mining concessions in Teleguay. And don't say I'm giving in to blackmail. All I'm doing is conceding to the inevitable.'

'I know.' She bit back a sigh. 'Will I always have to be watched over, Dad?'

'To some extent. But not by Mark, of course.'

'I should hope not! After the double role he played, I never want to see him again.'

'I understand how you feel,' her father soothed.

'You mean you—you know?'

'Of course. But he saved your life, my dear. Without him you'd be dead.'

Charlotte tossed her head. 'I'm still staggered you can forgive him.'

'I can forgive him anything for bringing you back safely.'

'But what if he repeats his behaviour with someone else he's engaged to protect—wouldn't you feel responsible?'

'He's assured me you're the last assignment he'll take.' Charles Beauville peered into her face. 'Why so sad, Sharly?'

'I'm thinking of Mark,' she admitted. 'Do the police have any idea that he——'

'All they know is that he's your chauffeur. And I've made it clear to the chief of police that no one's to know you were taken hostage. The less we're in the news, the better.'

'That should please Mark,' she said caustically.

'It does. Look, my dear, I know Mark blotted his copy-book over the kidnap, but he cleaned the page when he escaped with you. And his bravery in tackling Gizzer from the van was remarkable. Did you know the police wanted to take over, but he insisted on doing it himself? He seemed to think he was the only one who could stop the swine from shooting you first.'

Bitterness welled into Charlotte's throat. As she had anticipated, Mark's rescue of her had made him a hero. 'I still think he's despicable. I don't know how you can bear to talk to him. If I——'

The ringing of the telephone cut her short. It was Johnny, asking to see her, and, though the temptation to hide herself away from all men was strong, she knew she wouldn't forget Mark by hibernating.

'Give me a chance to rest for a few hours, Johnny,' she said. 'Then come on over.'

'Is he still top of your list?' her father queried as the call ended.

'Yes. I might even marry him.' She clasped her father round his waist. 'Oh, Dad, I do love you!'

'How strange!' He tapped the tip of her nose. 'Have another rest, my dear, and I'll see you later.'

When Charlotte finally entered the living-room—vibrant in a red-gold trouser suit that almost matched her hair—Johnny was ensconced in an armchair, chatting to her father. He came quickly across to her, his usually laconic greeting replaced by a fierce hug.

'Wonderful to see you, Sharly. Your father's been filling me in on the gory details.'

'They weren't all that gory!'

'Thanks to Mark,' her father added, and Johnny nodded agreement.

'I must say he put on a marvellous act, sir. I'd never have guessed what he was really up to.'

'He'll go on fooling people for the rest of his life,' Charlotte snapped, and, seeing the two men look at her in surprise, went into the garden.

It was a sultry evening, the slight breeze still sun-warmed. Where was Mark now? Free to set off on another nefarious scheme? Unlike her father, she didn't believe he'd ever play it straight.

She tried to blot out the passionate hours they had spent in the little bedroom in the farmhouse, but it would be easier to stop breathing! The memory of his touch, the feel of his hard body, his laboured breathing as he had fought and won control of himself, would haunt her for the rest of her days. If only he had taken her, accepted what she had willingly offered, she would at least have known the wonder of a perfect union. As it was, she was doomed to accept second best.

Turning to go indoors, she stopped as though dealt a body blow. She was dreaming! No, not a dream but a nightmare come to life. Yet not a nightmare either, but a reality, for the tall, supple-jointed man sauntering across the lawn was the one she had hoped never to see again. What effrontery he possessed to come here! What gall!

'Hello, Charlotte,' he said easily. 'I'm glad to see you're looking your old self again.'

'I feel my old self, too.'

She stared at him haughtily, though as he drew nearer she was shocked by his appearance. He was wearing the navy trousers and pale blue shirt in which he had been captured, but the trousers were torn and the shirt streaked with blood. His face was grey with fatigue, and a large purple bruise was swelling on his cheek, the colour echoing the dark shadows under his eyes. Her longing to cradle him close was so intense, she could only combat it with rage.

'How dare you come back here? Get out!'

'Charlotte!' Her father, having glimpsed Mark through the glass doors, was hurrying towards them. 'Whatever's got into you?'

'Do you need to ask?' she cried. 'How can you let him come here again?' She went to rush away, but Mark stepped into her path.

'Can't you forgive me, Charlotte?'

'Never.' From the corner of her eye she saw her father go inside. 'You might have conned Dad into forgiving you, but not me.'

'I don't see where conning comes into it. I did what I had to do.'

'For your beliefs, I presume?'

'Yes. But also because it was my job.'

'Is that all it was to you? A job? Oh, that makes you even more despicable!' She turned from him in anguish. 'Why have you come back?'

'To collect my things and talk to your father about us.'

'About *us*? You don't think I'd——' She choked on the words. 'You're insane! I told you in the farmhouse what I thought of you.'

'You can't mean it now! Dammit, Charlotte, you love me. The way you kissed me, let me touch you . . .'

'So what? I was scared for my life and—and you were available.' Digging her nails hard into her palms, she made her voice amused. 'All we have going for us is sex, and once the novelty wears off—as it will—you'd bore me silly. I'm astonished you can think otherwise.'

He had been grey-faced before, but now every vestige of colour seeped from his skin. He half turned, and as he did he saw Johnny in the doorway behind her.

'I suppose Johnny Craxton's more your type,' he said tonelessly.

'That's something I realised when I was a hostage,' she lied. 'I'm going to marry him.'

'Then there's no more for me to say. I hope you'll be happy, Charlotte. Now, if you'll excuse me, I'll say goodbye to your father and collect my things.'

With a shrug she turned away, not returning to the living-room until Mark had left it.

'I can't comprehend your attitude to Mark,' her father reproved. 'He risked his life to save you.'

'To save his own skin, you mean!' She flung out her hands in despair. 'He may have risked Gizzer's bullet, but that was only at the end, when he realised they'd be caught. If he had believed they would win, he'd have stuck with them. He's a traitor and a turncoat, Dad, and I can't forget it, even if you can!'

'A traitor?' Charles Beauville was bewildered and showed it. 'I know Mark was at fault in letting you give him the slip and going to the gallery on your own, but you were more to blame than he was. He and Sir Elrick both suggested you had three people watching you round the clock, but I didn't want to scare you and insisted on having only Mark.'

It was Charlotte's turn to be bewildered. 'What

does Sir Elrick have to do with it?'

'Mark works for him.'

'*Still*?'

'Naturally.' Her father frowned. 'I can't make you out. You act as if Mark should be sent to the Tower at the very least!'

'Forgive me butting in,' Johnny said diffidently, running his hand through his hair. 'But I get the feeling the two of you aren't on the same wavelength.' He focused on Charlotte. 'What have you got against Rayner?'

'He was in league with Parek.'

'My dear child!' Her father jumped from his chair as though he'd been shot. 'Don't you realise everything Mark did while you were both captive was to make Parek *think* he was on their side?'

'But he was!' she cried. 'He stopped me the first time I tried to escape! I heard what he said to them and I saw how he behaved.'

'He did it for your own safety. Gizzer was only a few feet away from you. Good grief, Sharly, Mark's a highly respected member of an organisation controlled by Sir Elrick.'

Speechless, Charlotte collapsed on a chair.

'Remember my mentioning General Rayner?' Johnny said to her. 'Well, Mark *is* his son.'

'His son? The one who went to Cuba?'

'That was an undercover job for the Americans,' her father interposed. 'And if there's anything else you'd like to know about him, you can ask Sir Elrick direct. He'll be spending the weekend with us. I want to thank him personally for letting us have Mark's services.'

Unsteadily Charlotte rose. 'Why didn't Mark tell me all this when were in the farmhouse?'

'He was afraid you'd inadvertently give him away.'

'But he could have told me when we were on the run!'

'I guess he had other things on his mind. If you——'

Not waiting to hear any more, Charlotte flew across the room. Only as she reached the door did she stop and fling out her hand to Johnny.

'It's no good,' she said breathlessly. 'I can't . . .'

'That's obvious,' he replied with a crooked grin. 'I knew it the moment Rayner walked in tonight.'

Giving him a fleeting smile, she raced up to Mark's room, praying he was still there. Without pausing to knock, she rushed in. He was snapping the lock shut on his case and he regarded her over the top of it.

'No more tantrums,' he bit out. 'I've had as much as I can take.'

She swallowed convulsively. 'Can you take an apology?'

'Apology?' His hand stilled on the case.

'Or do you want me to grovel at your feet? I'll willingly do so. And I'll stay there till you lift me up.' She went to kneel, but he caught her round the waist.

'No,' he said huskily. 'I prefer you to be on my level.' He bent closer. 'Why the change of heart?'

As she went to explain, he put his finger on her

lips. 'Later, my darling. For now, all I want is this.'

Drawing her close, he rested his cheek upon her hair, stroking the bright strands with an unsteady hand. Feeling his body tremble, tenderness surged through her.

'I love you so much, Mark. Can you forgive me for all the horrible things I said to you?'

'What things? All I recollect you saying is that you loved me!'

'You'll never know how much.'

'Then show me.'

Clasping her hands around his neck, she nestled into his body. His muscles tensed and she ran the tips of her fingers over his back. 'Scared of me?' she tantalised.

'Scared of myself. I've lived on my nerves for days, and holding you like this is putting a hell of a strain on them!'

'There's only one solution, then: you'll have to marry me quickly.'

Moving slightly back from her, he looked deep into her eyes, his own intent and serious. 'Will you expect me to give up my career and work for your father?'

She knew the answer to that instantly, but, not wishing him to think she was taking the question lightly, she took a moment to answer it. 'You'll always be your own man, Mark. That's one of the things I admire about you. So you must do whatever you want.'

'Can you see Charlotte Beauville's husband as an anonymous man with Security Intelligence?

Much as I'd like to carry on with my job, I'm afraid it won't be possible.'

'Does that make you unhappy?' she asked nervously.

Lowering his head, he delicately ran his tongue over her lips. 'It will have its compensations. But what about you? Still think I'm after your money?'

'Absolutely!'

They both laughed, and as she twined her arms round his neck again he prised them apart and led her firmly from the room. 'Control yourself, Miss Beauville. There's a little matter of your father's blessing and the marriage licence.'

Her chin lifted haughtily. 'You're bossing me again, Rayner!'

'You're quite right, miss. I am!'

THE COMPELLING AND UNFORGETTABLE SAGA OF THE CALVERT FAMILY

April	August	November
£2.95	£3.50	£3.50

From the American Civil War to the outbreak of World War I, this sweeping historical romance trilogy depicts three generations of the formidable and captivating Calvert women – Sarah, Elizabeth and Catherine.

The ravages of war, the continued divide of North and South, success and failure, drive them all to discover an inner strength which proves they are true Calverts.

Top author Maura Seger weaves passion, pride, ambition and love into each story, to create a set of magnificent and unforgettable novels.

W●RLDWIDE

Widely available on dates shown from Boots, Martins, John Menzies, W.H. Smith, Woolworths and other paperback stockists.

VOWS   *LaVyrle Spencer*   **£2.99**

When high-spirited Emily meets her father's new business rival, Tom, sparks fly, and create a blend of pride and passion in this compelling and memorable novel.

LOTUS MOON   *Janice Kaiser*   **£2.99**

This novel vividly captures the futility of the Vietnam War and the legacy it left. Haunting memories of the beautiful Lotus Moon fuel Buck Michael's dangerous obsession, which only Amanda Parr can help overcome.

SECOND TIME LUCKY   *Eleanor Woods*   **£2.75**

Danielle has been married twice. Now, as a young, beautiful widow, can she back-track to the first husband whose life she left in ruins with her eternal quest for entertainment and the high life?

These three new titles will be out in bookshops from September 1989.

W●RLDWIDE

Available from Boots, Martins, John Menzies, W.H. Smith, Woolworths and other paperback stockists.

Experience the thrill of 4 Mills & Boon Romances

An irresistible offer from Mills & Boon

Here's a personal invitation from Mills & Boon to become a regular reader of Romance. And to welcome you, we'd like you to have four books, an enchanting pair of glass oyster dishes and a special MYSTERY GIFT.

Then each month you could look forward to receiving 6 more brand – new Romances, delivered to your door, post and packing **free**. Plus our newsletter featuring author news, competitions and special offers.

This invitation comes with no strings attached. You can stop or suspend your subscription at any time, and still keep your **free** books and gifts.

It's so easy. Send no money now. Simply fill in the coupon below at once and post it to -

Reader Service, FREEPOST, P.O Box 236, Croydon, Surrey. CR9 9EL

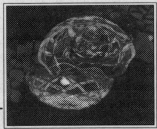

- ✂ - - - - - - - - - *No stamp required* - - - - - -

YES! Please rush me my 4 Free Romances and 2 FREE gifts!

Please also reserve me a Reader Service Subscription. If I decide to subscribe, I can look forward to receiving 6 brand new Romances each month, for just £8.10 delivered direct to my door. Post and packing is **free**. If I choose not to subscribe I shall write to you within 10 days - I can keep the books and gifts whatever I decide. I can cancel or suspend my subscription at any time.
I am over18.

EP61R

NAME ──────────────────────

ADDRESS ────────────────────

────────────────────────

─────────── *POSTCODE* ──────────

SIGNATURE ───────────────────

mps MAILING PREFERENCE SERVICE